Remaindered People
& Other Stories

Essential Prose Series 224

Canada Council   Conseil des arts
for the Arts   du Canada

ONTARIO ARTS COUNCIL
CONSEIL DES ARTS DE L'ONTARIO

an Ontario government agency
un organisme du gouvernement de l'Ontario

Ontario

Canada

Guernica Editions Inc. acknowledges the support of the Canada Council
for the Arts and the Ontario Arts Council. The Ontario Arts Council
is an agency of the Government of Ontario.
We acknowledge the financial support of the Government of Canada.

Remaindered People & Other Stories

Pratap Reddy

**GUERNICA
EDITIONS**
TORONTO · CHICAGO · BUFFALO · LANCASTER (U.K.)
2025

Guernica Founder: Antonio D'Alfonso

Michael Mirolla, general editor
Kulamrit Bamrah, editor
David Moratto, interior and cover design

Guernica Editions Inc.
1241 Marble Rock Rd., Gananoque, ON K7G 2V4
2250 Military Road, Tonawanda, N.Y. 14150-6000 U.S.A.
www.guernicaeditions.com

Distributors:
Independent Publishers Group (IPG)
600 North Pulaski Road, Chicago IL 60624
University of Toronto Press Distribution (UTP)
5201 Dufferin Street, Toronto (ON), Canada M3H 5T8

First edition.
Printed in Canada.

Legal Deposit—First Quarter
Library of Congress Catalog Card Number: 2024945870
Library and Archives Canada Cataloguing in Publication
Title: Remaindered people & other stories / Pratap Reddy.
Other titles: Remaindered people and other stories
Names: Reddy, Pratap, author
Series: Essential prose series ; 224.
Description: First edition. | Series statement: Essential prose series; 224
Identifiers: Canadiana (print) 20240455843 | Canadiana (ebook)
2024045586X | ISBN 9781771839365 (softcover) | ISBN 9781771839372 (EPUB)
Subjects: LCGFT: Short stories.
Classification: LCC PS8635.E337 R46 2025 | DDC C813/.6—dc23

For Peelu and Ramesh:
Sometimes ships sail away leaving
some passengers stranded on the shore

Contents

Sweet Memories

Through the small window of the basement room in which she was confined, she could see a patch of blue. A tiny piece of the sky. She felt a deep attachment to that only window in the room. Every now and then it drew her eyes, like a magnet.

The window was in the top right-hand corner, like a postage stamp, and the long grey wall may well have been an envelope. Together they seemed to bear the only news from the outside world—a passing cloud, a bird perched on the sill, a bee on its daily rounds.

In the spring, a nearby maple would rear its head to peep into the room. Bunches of its new leaves could be seen just above the window's lower frame. Like a trickle of letters, spelling the name of the country on the stamp. Sometimes it seemed to read India, as if the envelope brought tidings from home.

In the summer, when the foliage had grown thicker the leaves would spell ... well ... maybe Indonesia. What news could she expect from that archipelago in the Indian Ocean? She hardly knew anybody there.

For that matter how many people did she know in India now? Only a handful. Many she knew were dead, her husband included. Some had drifted away—like her daughter, vowing never to reconcile. Whether dead or estranged, they inhabited the pages of her precious photo album, her only link to the past.

Now it was late fall. The tree outside had shed all its yellow and brown leaves, and a couple of twigs could be seen. What countries were spelled with three or four letters?

Chad. Laos. Iran. Iraq. She had been good at geography when she was in school. That was years and years ago. And it meant nothing to anybody. She was a girl, after all. It was more important that she knew how to make shapely rotis and churn curd to make butter. But it came in handy, her fascination with the atlas, when she had to tutor Hemanth when he was in elementary school. But these countries did not evoke any excitement in her ...

Then she got it. She knew what the twigs spelled: USA. The land of the free. The land of plenty. Where her second cousin and her large brood lived in such obvious prosperity. Her cousin had sent her photographs of their family holidays in California or Florida—she could never remember which—with sweeps of blue in the background. The sky and the sea. So deep and so bright, as if they used an entirely different colour palette down there.

In the winter, especially when it was snowing, no alphabets suggested themselves to form the name of any country. It kind of summed up of her situation: a stateless person. She was an expatriate and was neither a permanent resident nor a citizen of Canada. Her son had lured her to the country, dangling before her the carrot of a better life.

She got up with the gawky movements of a string puppet and went into an inner room. She opened cupboards, drawers, suitcases, and after rummaging for a while with rising desperation, she at last found the object of her quest. Her photo album. Her most treasured possession which had *Sweet Memories* written in gold on the cover. She carried it to the front room, and seating herself on the bed, began to leaf through it.

Many of the early snaps were in black and white. And small, having been taken with a box camera by her husband. She chuckled at the old photographs of her friends and herself dressed in fashions gone by, fashions flaunted by film actresses like Savitri and Jamuna. There were so many pictures, so many faces with smiles frozen on them. It was as if there was no place for grief in her album. It troubled her that she could not recall the names of some of the people in the photographs. Maybe it was a sign of advancing age. She was nearly seventy.

Then she stopped turning the pages and frowned. There was something she was supposed to do. A clear instruction her jailor daughter-in-law had given her before locking her up. Only it was not so clear now. She groped in her mind but couldn't put a finger to it. She gave a shrug and tossed the thought out of her mind, telling herself, "Who cares?"

She smiled when she saw the childhood pictures of her son Hemanth: Hemu on a tricycle, Hemu eating an ice cream cone, Hemu dressed like Superman. When she came upon a grown-up Hemanth with his wife, her smile evaporated, curling her lips downward. She shut the album with a slap.

She stared into space, but her eyes were trained inward on some joyless corner of her mind. Then her eyes moved to the window high up on the wall. How inviting the pale blue sky was, with no clouds to mar its beauty. It hinted at the limitless expanse of the universe, a promise of unfettered freedom. She shot up from the bed and walked purposefully, if unsteadily, to the front door and tried to open it. When it didn't, she rattled the door in annoyance. She then banged a tattoo on the door with increasing violence and stopped only when her clenched fist began to hurt.

She went back to the bed and lay down in quiet misery. For a prisoner, her life was not uncomfortable. Her bed was six inches of memory foam. Back home in India she had slept on a thin, loosely stuffed cotton mattress. In the summer, she would lay herself down on the bare floor, feeling the delicious cool of the stone on her uncovered midriff, between the hemline of the blouse and the fold of her sari. She would rest her head on the crook of her arm, disdaining the pillow which would have been slow-cooked in the heat of the day.

She had to admit she was not a captive in the real sense of the term. More like someone under house arrest. Not for a full twenty-four hours a day either. Yet it was more shameful to her than a life sentence for a heinous crime. What would her friends and relatives back home think? It was a mercy she couldn't recall their names.

* * *

"How lucky you are, Saraswati!" they had said, her neighbours, her distant relatives, her servant maid, the milkman, the greengrocer who came on a bicycle, the shopkeeper down the road who was known to use fraudulent weights on his scales. Some said it with honest admiration, some with envy, some with plain bad grace.

Hemanth was coming any day now to take her to Canada. All the formalities were over, he had said over the phone. Just as well. How many forms she had signed, reams and reams of them! She felt happy, fortunate and even blessed to have a son like Hemanth. Going to live in the West brought a lot of prestige to her and the family. But it was not all unalloyed happiness. Leaving the country meant breaking bonds, and in her case, she would be putting half the globe between herself and her discontented daughter. All said and done, Canada was not exactly a big draw either. All those pictures of snowbound landscapes she saw in calendars and Christmas cards made her shiver.

She had gone to the airport in a taxi to receive her son, taking a couple of neighbours with her. Some of the younger men from the neighbourhood came along too, packing themselves into a hired minivan. Hemanth emerged from the terminal building like some butterfly out of a chrysalis. He looked different from the swirling mass of humanity around him, and not just to her doting maternal eyes. He had that sheen that brown people acquire after having lived in the temperate zone for a few years. The cut and colour of his clothes were a bit off too, but they had an expensive look about them even if they had been picked up in a sale.

The boisterous young neighbours draped a rose and lily garland around Hemanth's neck and pressed a matching nosegay into his hands. They formed a sedan-chair with two men interlocking their arms and carried an embarrassed looking Hemanth to the parking lot. While the people around rolled their eyes or smirked, in Saraswati's eyes there was nothing but love and admiration for her son.

In the two weeks he spent in India, he bought her new clothes and had painters apply a new coat to the house. They emptied the place, getting rid of unwanted things by selling them or donating them to servants, so that the new owner could move in.

She boarded the plane, her heart full of joy and ex-pectation, and a twinge of nervousness too. It was the first time she was travelling by air. But with her son sitting next to her she felt secure. He showed her how to buckle the seat belt and how to release the swing-back table and summoned the cabin crew when she felt thirsty.

Her daughter-in-law and granddaughter were at the airport to receive them. Even though it was spring, the day was cold and grey, with clouds massed like a shroud over-head. It had stopped raining, but there was a steady breeze blowing and the roads were still wet. Dank trees stood glumly along the way.

The first few weeks of her life in the western world were full of gratifying discoveries: the relative cleanliness, the sense of abundance, the semblance of efficiency that everything around her had. Of course, things were not as convenient as they were back home in India, where you could find servants, cheap transport, and helpful neigh-bours. And you never felt lonely or unsafe there—a com-forting buzz of life surrounded you wherever you went.

Here everyone left the house all at once when it struck eight of a weekday morning, leaving her behind in the silent empty house like a piece of furniture. She learned to while away her time doing some cleaning and cooking. This state of uneasy bliss lasted for a few weeks.

One day her son Hemanth took her aside and said, "Amma, I want to speak to you."

"What is it, Hemu?" She expected her son to complain about her cooking. She suspected her daughter-in-law, who was always moaning about grocery bills, disapproved of her making so many dishes even though Hemanth seemed to enjoy eating them.

Her son looked acutely embarrassed, but overcoming his emotions, he told her how to correctly use the commode in the washroom and how to clean herself afterwards. Though everyone knew you did them differently in India, her son's unwelcome tutorial made her feel small. Years ago, she had potty-trained Hemanth herself before he started nursery school, telling him he was a big boy now.

Life had come full circle. But it didn't end there.

A few days later, her son confronted her again. "Amma ..." he started saying.

"Hemu, I know, I know. Give me some time. It's not easy to learn new ways of doing things. Especially at my age ..."

"It's just not that, Amma," Hemanth said.

"Tell Prabha, I'm sorry. I have become so forgetful nowadays. I will learn to adjust. Everything is new to me here. Give me some time."

But to her surprise and horror, they moved her from the guest bedroom to the basement. She had never heard of basements in India. As far as she knew nobody lived underground.

When Hemanth brought her two suitcases and set them down, Saraswati mustered enough spirit to declare, "I want to go back to India."

"Don't be unreasonable, Amma. Where will you live in India?"

"Don't be unreasonable!" Saraswati's voice quavered. She was torn between intense rage and an impulse to sob. "I was living so comfortably in my own house. You've brought me here and placed me in this hellhole."

"The suite is quite nice. I could get at least six hundred dollars a month if I rented it out."

"Then why don't you? I don't want to live in Canada, I don't want this nice suite either. I know your dad's pension may not be much, but I can live at an old age home or an ashram in India."

"Amma, believe me, all that is easier said than done. At least in Canada we are here for you."

"You are here for me?! Your sister may not be there for me but at least she didn't ill-treat me ..."

Her voice had become hoarse, and tears formed in her eyes. If she uttered another word, she knew she would break down. Hemanth turned his back and went up the stairs.

She could never understand how or why her beloved son had turned so hard-hearted. Most probably it was Prabha, her wily daughter-in-law, who manipulated him into doing things he wouldn't have done. Prabha wouldn't have relished the idea of her moving to Canada. An extra mouth to feed, she would have reckoned.

Yes, Prabha must be behind all this. Saraswati remembered how one day when she was going about the house cleaning, dusting, and generally looking around, Prabha had come home early from work and found her in the master bedroom.

"What are you doing, Amma?" Prabha had said sharply. "Can I help you?"

"Er … I was looking for my rosary. I can't find it anywhere."

Prabha didn't seem convinced. Saraswati got the impression that she suspected her of going through her things. "I don't know where it is. But it couldn't be in my cupboard. I'll ask Hemanth when he comes home," Prabha said.

That must be it!

* * *

The patch of sky turned into a darker shade of blue—peacock-blue—with a hint of gold from the setting sun. It looked, not like a postage stamp, but like a folded silk sari with gold embroidery along the edge. Like the sari she had worn for her daughter's wedding. The function had been an expensive affair—inviting five hundred guests was no small matter. People congratulated her, amazed that she could pull it off almost single-handedly. But most of her savings had gone up in smoke, like the sandalwood kindling in the sacred fire.

Five years later, when her son-in-law lost his job, he asked her for a loan. She had to refuse. What little remained in the bank was to pay for Hemanth's higher education. Deeply offended, her son-in-law broke all contact, and forbade his wife from visiting her.

Suddenly, she heard sounds coming from beyond the door. Voices, and a clinking noise. Then the sound of a key turning in the lock.

* * *

Hemanth unlocked the door that led to the basement. Pushing open the door which squealed as if in pain, Hemanth went down the long flight of stairs. He was followed by his wife Prabha and their seven-year-old daughter, Asmita. Hemanth and Prabha had the patina of tiredness which comes from putting in long gruelling hours. Their daughter, who had been talking excitedly about her adventures at school and at daycare, fell silent.

In the surreal half-light of the basement, Hemanth saw his mother seated on the couch, rocking back and forth and muttering to herself. Inky shadows lapped around her.

"Who are you?" his mother said, looking at them as if with unseeing eyes.

"How are you feeling, Amma?" Hemanth asked.

The little girl walked up and said, as she had been tutored to, "I love you, Grandma." She planted a kiss gingerly on the bemused old woman's cheek.

"I want you all to leave the house at once," Saraswati said, "or I'll call my son who lives upstairs."

Prabha toggled an electrical switch, and there was an explosion of light in the small room. Saraswati shielded her eyes with the palm of her hand.

"Have you taken your medicine?" Prabha asked, exchanging worried looks with Hemanth.

Hemanth sat down next to his mother. He had grown inured to the wanderings of his mother's addled mind. Unless she took her tablets in a timely manner, her mind tended to lose its grip on reality.

Hemanth took her hand in his and said, "We are friends of your son who lives upstairs."

Saraswati unexpectedly began to sob. She said, "I am a prisoner here."

"We are in the same boat," Hemanth said under his breath.

He had sold his share of his dad's small house and had given up a manager's position to migrate to Canada. Now he was working as a labourer in a warehouse, and his wife as a cashier in a coffee shop. All the money they made went into the mortgage, auto insurance, daycare for his daughter, and his mother's medical bills. When they bought the house, it had seemed like a smart move. They had figured that instead of paying rent they could make payments towards the mortgage and at the same time build equity in their home. They had also counted on renting out their basement, but that plan fell through when his mother came to stay.

There was no way they could all go back to India and seamlessly resume their lives there. He would never be able to get his job back and real estate prices would have shot up beyond his reach. Besides, there was no such thing as a dependable old age pension or universal healthcare over there.

"I wanted to go out so much. But the door was locked," said Saraswati.

"Don't you worry, I'll take you out for a drive. But you will have to take your medicine first," Hemanth said. Prabha had brought a glass of water, and a tablet on a saucer.

"You are a kind man," his mother said. She looked into Hemanth's face, and asked, "Would you lock up your mother?"

"No," he lied, squeezing her hand.

"But my son does."

"Perhaps he's worried," Hemanth said, "that you will wander off and lose your way."

One evening when they returned home from work, they had found Saraswati missing. They'd run hither and thither, fearing for her, fearful of the authorities, until they located her, cowering in a nearby bus stop shelter. While it was a relief not having to call 911, they realized it was unwise to leave her all alone in their two-storey home. The only practical solution was to confine her to the basement.

When his mother was suspected of having early stages of dementia, Hemanth had brought her to Canada on a long-term visitor's visa as it would have taken forever to get her permanent residence. But it meant she didn't qualify for state medical insurance.

Saraswati swallowed the tablet that Prabha gave her and returned the glass with shaking hands.

"Prabha will make some tea for us. Once we have it we'll go for a drive on the Lakeshore Road. It will be so beautiful at this time of the day. Wouldn't you like that?"

"Yes, that will be nice."

Remaindered People

I was down and out in Mumbai when the offer came. And mind you, it was in the nick of time. I had been fired from my copywriter's job and soon afterwards was dumped by Tina, my girlfriend of six months. I couldn't even afford the rent for my digs and my life savings were at rock bottom.

An old college mate called me from Ottawa—or Oshawa, or some other place in Canada just as freezing, I'm sure. Would I care to return to Hyderabad to keep an eye on his aged and ailing dad?

"You don't have to really take care of him, you know," Vikram said. "Just be around. You'll have a nice bedroom with an attached bath, and anyway, you can have the same food the cook makes for Dad."

"What kind of food, Vik?" I asked, suddenly alert. Goodness knows what doctor-advised pap the old geezer must be consuming.

"Normal Indian stuff, man. You don't have to worry on that score. You remember our old cook Rajamma, don't you? She's still alive and cooking. Come on Brij, free board and lodging. Just think about it. Nothing to be sneezed at ... in the circumstances."

"What circumstances?" I asked.

"Word spreads." Vik sighed. "While I'm sorry about your job, but from what I heard, you are better off without that floozie."

"For a person who's looking for favours you must watch your tongue, bro."

My friend chuckled. I hadn't heard from him for aeons. People don't keep in touch with guys they reckon as having little usefulness down the road. My misfortunes somehow raised my worth in Vik's esteem. His offer was like a godsend at that point in my life. For free board and lodging I wouldn't have minded keeping both my eyes on his father. Though I remembered Vik's dad as a Tartar, a tall and unsmiling person.

And that's how I found myself in a wheezing autorickshaw, trundling up a narrow shady road in Jubilee Hills in the company of two battered suitcases and an old box guitar—the sum total of all my worldly possessions.

I paid off the fare (a good portion of what remained of my lifetime earnings) to the surly, betel-chewing autorickshaw driver and pushed open the small pedestrian-only sheet metal gate. The big-brother gate, which was reserved for four-wheelers, was secured with a chain and a lock from the inside.

The deceptively small house had the aspect of a cottage, with sloping roofs, stone facings and window boxes overflowing with flowers. The house was surrounded by gawky, adolescent trees, planted only after the house was built on the lot. A lawn, painstakingly kept emerald green

with large doses of scarce water, had lantana bushes running along three sides.

The front door was opened by Rajamma. "You are Brij-
babu, aren't you?" she said with a smile, peering through
her thick glasses which sat askew on the bridge of her nose.
"Ayya is having a nap now. I'll take you to your room."

The bedroom upstairs was nothing like my pad. The
hovel I had rented was small, ill-ventilated, and with
Turner-like artwork on the walls produced by seeping mois-
ture from Mumbai's monsoon. But this room was big and
bright, with tall windows and a door leading to a balcony. I
took my meagre belongings and stored them in the ward-
robe. I had a quick bath and went downstairs.

Rajamma had laid out a simple meal: boiled rice,
mouth-wateringly aromatic sambar, vegetables, papad, a
variety of relishes, and cake-solid yoghurt. I had not had
such tasty home-cooked food in a very long time. My
mother used to cook such meals, but now she lived in the
USA taking care of my elder sister's children. My father had
died young, so my mother brought us up single-handedly,
and had to sell the small property we owned to get my
sister married.

Nowadays my mother hardly ever visited India. She
would have come more often had I a steady job or continued
to live in any one city and rented a decent place. My mother
used to say that I changed jobs like they were shirts. (Poor
lady, she had no clue how often I changed clothes.)

After I finished my lunch, I went back to my bedroom.
I tried to read a few pages of a new much-hyped book which
Tina had succeeded in making me buy. Wondering what
Tina would be up to at that moment in Mumbai, I fell asleep.

I woke from my siesta and tarried in the luxurious bed, feeling like a millionaire. I wished Tina could see this. Downstairs, tea and snacks were waiting for me. How different from the thimbleful of acrid chai my ex-employer doled out in chipped china.

As the day stretched ahead of me, I wondered as to how I would spend my time. Not just that afternoon but in the days to come. Reading, perhaps. But I hadn't spotted any book cupboard in the house. I wondered if there even was one. Old Vik never sounded like a walking encyclopaedia. For him, Tom Clancy had been the high watermark of literature.

TV was a definite no-no. I didn't have the nerve to turn on the one I had seen in the formal drawing room. It was humongous and presided over a sofa set of carved teak with burgundy and gold upholstery. I wouldn't want the seat of my trousers to dirty the sofas.

Since I was a self-taught musician, I could always strum away on my out-of-tune guitar, and learn a few more songs to add to my small repertoire ...

It was then that a long-cherished idea resurfaced: I must start my own blog. It was my longstanding grouse that I would have done so already but for the demands on my time and energy from my boss and Tina.

What would I write about? The life of an itinerant jingle-maker could provide rich material, I was sure. What about resources? That was the real catch. There were monthly fees for good blog hosts and I didn't have a paystub turning up in my office mail month after month. Besides, the house was not even hooked up to the internet, and the old boy downstairs seemed to be in no urgent need of it. Unless he wanted to order a coffin online. Maybe I could learn to mine Vik for all his worth. He was the one with deep pockets. I didn't see anything wrong in making Vik pay for the internet. You scratch my back, and I'll scratch yours (or your dad's, for that matter).

* * *

Later in the evening Rajamma led me into the holy-of-holies. Vik's father was lying in a big bed, all bundled up. The room was dark, the window-curtains closed. There was a smell of pain balm with an undertone of Savlon-like antiseptic.

"How was your journey, Brijmohan?" the old man asked in a quavering voice. He was the only one I knew who used the long form of my name instead of the diminutive Brij, and yet he somehow managed to make me feel like a shorty. I remembered him towering over my frail, small frame, even after I had grown to my full extent. I stood five-six in my slippers.

We indulged in small talk. "I'm doing nothing as of now," I said, in answer to one of his questions. "I might look for a job in a local advertising agency once I settle in."

"There aren't many ad firms round about here. Mumbai is the Mecca for advertising."

"Unfortunately so," I said. Time hadn't marred his style of speaking—a string of edicts directed at lesser mortals. "I hope to find something here. Not necessarily a big break, you know, something that will keep me occupied and provide me with some pocket money."

"You must be more ambitious in life, Brijmohan," Vik's dad said.

I squirmed and said nothing. Soon the third-degree interrogation came to an end, and wishing him goodnight, I left with a sense of relief. Vik's dad and his room spooked me.

The evening was still young. I sat in a cane armchair on the verandah and tried to read the morning's newspaper. It felt like eating cold toast. As I didn't have the guts to switch on the monster TV in the drawing room, I went for a stroll.

Jubilee Hills was a nice posh area. Most of the houses had well-laid-out gardens in the front. Quite a few houses were built like mini-palaces, gaudy and ostentatious. But just as many were small and pretty, nestling amongst flowering-shrubs and fruit-trees. Here and there were Gurkhas in their khaki uniforms standing guard at the houses. If I lingered too long in front of a house, even if there were no Gurkhas to give inimical stares, an Alsatian or a Doberman would bound up to the gate and bark up-roariously until I got going again.

On my way back, I got an idea for the theme of my blog. I could write about my life in Vik's ailing dad's house and give it a catchy title like "Keeper of the Dying." A title which could make even the dead sit up. Something that would knock people's socks off. I reasoned the blog had the poten-tial to become quite popular. A ringside, or rather bedside, view of a person on his last legs. And with a little bit of luck, the old boy might literally die in my arms. Just imagine capturing it on live camera. Boy, what copy it would make! Talk about going viral. Suddenly, I felt chuffed. It was a feel-ing I had not experienced in a long while. But when the thought crossed my mind that the original scheme had Vik paying for the blog site, it put a slight damper on things. But not for very long. A writer needed to be opportunistic, like Hemingway. Writing was not for the squeamish.

When I returned, it was dusk already. I was sorely tempted to turn on the TV which stood like a silent monument in the living room. But thinking better of it, I went up to my room. As there was no internet, my laptop remained packed. I had not yet activated my mobile for pecuniary reasons. I wished Vik's dad could give me a stipend, in addition to free board and lodging. (I know, hope springs eternal.)

I picked up the novel which Tina had recommended and began to read. It put me to sleep in a blink. So much for hype.

* * *

While I felt fortunate about my lotus-eater life in a way, I found it hard to kill time. With Rajamma's help I located a book cupboard in one of the rooms. Most of the books were medical in nature but for laymen. There were a few writers of yesteryears such as Harold Robbins and Irving Wallace stuck between *Reader's Digest* publications on self-improvement. I picked up Leon Uris's *Topaz*, hoping it would be an exciting read, and it being a thickish book, was sure to occupy a few hours of my idle life.

The next evening, after returning from my ramble through the narrow winding bylanes of Jubilee Hills, I made myself bold and knocked on the old man's half-open door.

"Come in."

When I pushed open the door, the room was silent and almost totally dark. Vik's dad was absently staring at the TV which had its volume turned down. The dancing images of the TV were reflected on his face. Eerie.

"Uncle, would you mind if I watched TV in the drawing room?"

"Go ahead," he said in his deep voice. "You don't have to ask my permission to use anything in this house. Think of it as your own."

I was pleased, although for one terrifying moment a thought had passed through my mind that he might invite me to join him in watching TV in his sepulchral room, rather than have two TVs going at the same time. To give the devil his due, Vik's dad was anything but niggardly.

"Thank you, Uncle!" I said.

I may have sounded a bit too enthusiastic, because he said, "As long as you don't make a nuisance of yourself, Brijmohan."

I turned on the antique set, and it jumped to life with a lot of crackle and flashes of light. I surfed the channels before settling for *The Big Bang Theory*. After that I watched the late-night news and then went to bed.

* * *

As days rolled by, I began to miss the internet. I decided I must get a connection by hook or by crook. But I didn't know how—meaning I didn't know who'd foot the bill. Should I ask Vik right away or wait a few weeks? I didn't want to sound too demanding or greedy. I'd rather not kill the golden goose, I thought. It was still too early.

The routine suited me fine in many ways. The rest was doing me good, and I didn't look as tired. (Tina often used to say, with disapproval in her voice, that I looked as if hadn't slept well the previous night.) Besides, I was catching up on reading, too, running through the collection in the book cupboard quite fast.

In the first few days, my interaction with Vik's dad was minimal. He remained in his room during the day, with Rajamma taking meals, tea or coffee to his room at odd times—I guess whenever he wanted them rather than following a fixed schedule. Sometimes I could hear him move about on the ground floor of the house in the middle of the night like a nocturnal prowler.

* * *

While I was more than satisfied with the unruffled tenor of my new life, there was one aspect which made me slightly uncomfortable: Vik' dad and I were like strangers in a mansion and there was no Hitchcock at hand to stir things up a bit. I don't quite know if it was the lack of having someone—other than servants—to talk to or if it was some kind of pity I felt for the loaded but lonely invalid, which goaded me into action.

One evening, on impulse, I went up to Vik's dad's room and asked him if he would like to watch TV in the hall with me. He was lying on his side, his face turned away from the bedroom TV which was spewing its fare to a phantom audience. I felt a bit stupid for asking. He already had a TV switched on, so why would he bother to crawl out of his dungeon?

He turned in the bed to face me. After a few moments, he mumbled something. I thought he was berating me, and I started to beat a hasty retreat. But he raised himself, and then reached for his walking stick. He got, up and started shuffling after me—I could almost hear the ropes and pulleys in his body groaning.

In the drawing room, I approached the TV, and asked affably, "What program would you like to watch, Uncle?"

"Whatever you are interested in. I'm indifferent to all of them." Rich, coming from a person who has the TV in his room on for almost 24/7. Or maybe not—the switched-on TV was perhaps a stand-in for some live human company. I turned on the TV, and it broke explosively into a jingle in Hindi with manic accompaniment of a hundred musical instruments.

"Is this the kind of things you do for a living?"

"Pretty much," I said. "Only, I write in English."

He mimicked, recalling a jingle from his salad days about a popular local cola: *"Happy days are here again, Thums Up! Thums Up!"*

I hoped the jingle was a random choice rather than an oblique reference to my new parasitic lifestyle.

He sat through the episode of the serial which was about two warring business houses where the CEOs, CFOs, their wives, and their maids were all involved in corporate shenanigans. Vik's dad took it all in without a complaint. But when the program ended, he refused to stay back to watch the late-night news in English.

"The things these politicians do, it will only make my blood boil. Good night and thank you for the ... er ... outing." He got up awkwardly and hobbled away.

From then onwards we watched TV together in the living room every night. He didn't mind whichever program I put on. He sat through them mostly in companionable silence, grimacing occasionally at the antics of the actors.

One evening, as we sat in front of the TV watching a movie about cybercrime, I said, "Uncle, we should get an internet connection."

"Why? I have no interest in the world around me what-soever. I have a TV and a phone which are bad enough."

"I was thinking of setting up Skype on my laptop. You could see Vikram or Ananya while you're speaking to them. It's like a phone and a camera rolled into one. But you need the internet for that."

"If they so desperately want to see me, would they have left me to rot here in the first place?"

"You can't blame them, Uncle. Take Ananya, for in-stance. Once girls get married, they move into their in-laws' home, and follow their husbands wherever they go—even to Timbuktu if need be. How can you blame Ananya?"

"Point taken about Anni. What about Vikki?"

"Everybody who has talent goes West, Uncle. That's where the opportunities lie. Only the dross get left behind! Like yours truly. By the way, didn't you ever want to go and live with Vikki or Anni?"

"One of them lives in Canada and the other in Norway, if you please! The weather there is unbearable for the bet-ter part of the year. I visited each of them and stayed for a few months. I was confined to the house most of the time as they are all so busy. I felt like a prisoner there. I thought I'd go crazy if I had to live there forever."

"Oh," I said, seeing the prospect of an internet connec-tion disappear like landscape in a Canadian or Norwegian whiteout.

"I know what you are thinking," Vik's dad said, looking at me suspiciously. "'This man spends most of his time holed up in his bedroom, so how is that different?' Well, for one thing, it's my choice. And for another, things are differ-ent here. There are servants to help you. And I am mobile. I have a car and can get hold of a chauffeur anytime I want."

"You are right, Uncle," I said. "Having put in years of service, you are entitled to choose your lifestyle. But what will happen when you grow old and are not able take care of yourself?"

"Yes, that's a terrible prospect, especially for those whose children live abroad. Old age homes are our ultimate refuge, I suppose. We are past our prime and have limited utility. Nobody really wants us—like books which have no takers. We are remaindered people."

One evening I asked Vik's dad whether he would care to join me for an evening stroll.

"I can barely walk up to the front door without having to stop a dozen times to recover my breath. I'll needlessly slow you down."

"Let that not bother you, Uncle. If you feel too tired, we can always turn back."

For the first few days Vik's dad found the going diffi-cult and always demanded that we return even before we reached the main road. He complained of joint pains and muscle cramps but that did not deter him from accompany-ing me in my rambles. By and by his stamina improved, and soon he got rid of his walking stick altogether.

He began to truly enjoy the evening constitutional, and the accompanying conversation even more so, I felt. He would talk at length about his career in the government, the showdowns he had with his superiors, and the holidays they took to almost every nook and cranny of India when Vik and Ananya were children. For my part, I too had much to say—about my life in Mumbai and my two exes: my ob-noxious boss and the faithless Tina.

Vik's dad said, "Don't brood over your past, Brijmohan. Always look to the future, you're still young. One never knows why things happen the way they do. As they say in Telugu: *Antha mana manchike*. Everything happens for our good. Even if it doesn't appear so at the time."

As days passed our walks became longer, and took more than an hour to complete. When we returned to our base it was I who felt more pooped out than my walking mate. Vik's dad would cast a sidelong glance at me, a shadow of a smile hovering on his lips.

Just before dinnertime, it became a routine for Vik's dad to head for his rosewood wine cabinet and, like a magician pulling a rabbit out of his hat, pluck a bottle of aperitif—something like Calvados or Dubonnet. It was the most anticipated moment of the day for me. We would sit in the living room before the TV, nursing the drinks as they say, and idly chatting, indifferent to the grisly dramas being played out on the idiot box.

After we had a drink or two, we would move to the dining room. Under a many-branched Bohemian chandelier, two places were set on a long shining teakwood table which had eight plush chairs arranged around it. Like many an object in the house, they had been hitherto condemned to neglect and disuse. Vik's dad started having all his meals at the dining table again, often in my company. Rajamma stopped taking trays to his bedroom.

One day, as we were having dinner, he told Rajamma, "Why don't you make bitter gourd curry one of these days? I've not had it in a long time."

Pat came Rajamma's reply: "Brij-babu does not like bitter gourd."

That was true, but I started to protest: "I don't mind ..."

"If that's the case," Vic's dad said tamely, "then it's fine. You don't have to make it."

I didn't know whether to feel horrified or touched.

* * *

Unlike Mumbai, jobs in Hyderabad were scarce in the creative field. When I heard of an opportunity at a small advertising firm, I sent in my application, taking pains to add Vik's dad's name as my reference. He was well-known, had connections, and was a member of prestigious clubs. I got a call.

On the day of the interview, I got up early, and after getting into my Sunday best, I went down for breakfast.

"My! How nice you look when you wear fine clothes!" Rajamma said. But she was quick to catch on. "Do you have an interview for a job or something?"

"Yes."

"Before you leave, don't neglect to say your prayers," she said, pointing to the Pooja-room which was tenanted by half-a-dozen silver statuettes of Hindu gods, trapped in an atmosphere of soot and smoke.

On the morning of the very first interview I attended after the completion of my master's program in English Literature, my mother had made me stand before a picture of the blindfolded Balaji, a Hindu deity, and pray. She put the sacred red dot on my forehead which I wiped off as soon as I stepped out of the house.

This one, too, like most of the job interviews I went to in my life, didn't seem promising.

The HR manager said, his voice devoid of any enthusiasm, "We will let you know. It may take three to four weeks."

"Three to four weeks!"

The manager narrowed his eyes and said, "You should learn to wait, young man."

"They also serve who stand and wait," I silently mis-quoted to myself, and put the matter out my mind.

One evening as we were sauntering past a roadside internet kiosk which proclaimed in gory red lettering Rs 15/- an hour, Vik's dad said, "We should get an internet connection. I don't mind paying for it. You look so bored with life. You obviously need something to do. Like starting on your bogs or whatever."

"Blogs, Uncle," I said, laughing. "I only hope they don't turn out to be shitty!"

"And what was that telephone thing—sky or something? We should get that, too."

"Skype," I said. "It is a great way to keep in touch." I must have sounded like a copywriter making up taglines for newfangled ways of communicating.

"You know, Brij, people say we are more connected today because of new technologies. Wired world and all that. In our time, we used stuff like inland letters and telegrams. But were we less connected then? I think not. We were there for one another, sharing our joys and sorrows, not just holiday pictures."

"You're probably right, Uncle."

I contacted the dealer of a company called Hathaway and arranged for a connection. I couldn't understand why anyone would call an internet provider after Shakespeare's wife. Even more surprising was Vik's dad's take. "Maybe they've named it after that lovely young British actress." Watching TV 24/7, one comes to know of things, I supposed.

I emailed old Vik about setting up Skype, and taking Ananya's telephone number from Vik's dad, I telephoned her in Norway to tell her about my plan for a Skype call. It was almost midnight there, but I didn't care. Norway was the Land of the Midnight Sun, after all.

Neither did Ananya: "Such a good idea! It's so nice of you to think of it."

So, on the day of Diwali, when the firecrackers were exploding all round, making Hyderabad sound like an embattled city, we made the calls. It was midmorning in Oslo, and the previous night in Oshawa, the city where Vik lived.

Vik's dad was overjoyed to see and talk to Anni, his two granddaughters and his dutiful son-in-law. Vik didn't sound too pleased to be yanked out of his bed to listen to Diwali greetings from his dad.

"I don't know what's wrong with that fellow. He didn't seem too happy to talk to me."

"It's two o'clock in the night for him, Uncle. He has to go to work in the morning."

In the evening, I helped Rajamma light clay lamps on the window ledges and the parapet of the terrace. The house looked lovely, outlined as it were with light.

As we stood on the flat roof, under the moonless sky, watching fireworks light up the night, Rajamma said, "It's years since the house looked so festive, so joyful. Not since Amma passed away, and that was nearly ten years ago."

* * *

One afternoon I got the call from the ad agency—earlier than expected and one could guess why. To cut a long story short, I didn't get the job. Truth to tell, my skill set and what was required of the candidate didn't match. But that didn't make my disappointment any less acute. I didn't get out of bed until noon. For some reason, memories of my affair with Tina were reawakened. It wasn't easy to get her out of my system. Any surprise that I would sometimes jokingly call her my Taenia Solium? By now, Tina would have hitched onto someone with better prospects.

Fate had always dealt me a loser's hand. What else could you expect when the god who presided over my destiny hid his eyes from the world?

As I was having lunch, Rajamma asked me if I was ill. "Last night I sat up late working on my laptop," I said.

"You have been looking very tired in the last few days. Is everything all right?"

"Yes," I said, lying.

"What about the job? Did you get it?" Rajamma would have made a killing as a mind reader.

"No, Rajamma. I didn't come up to their expectations."

"What nonsense. I'll talk to Ayya. He knows a lot of people. He can put in a word for you."

A few days later as I was having an early lunch, Rajamma said that Vik's dad was expecting a visitor at seven in the evening, and he would like me to meet him.

The guest arrived on the dot. Vik's dad greeted him. "Welcome, Chaudhury-garu. This is Brij, my son's best friend." There was enthusiastic handshaking all around.

The guest had an aura of success about him, accentuated by his gold tiepin and cufflinks. The fragrance of Polo preceded him like a vanguard wherever he went. I was my usual unkempt self, faded jeans and a loose rumpled T-shirt with a smutty message, mercifully faded, printed on the front. Vik's dad had exchanged his usual, crumpled kurta-pajamas for an ironed bush shirt and trousers.

Eating Rajamma's brinjal bajjies with Maggi tomato ketchup, Vik's dad and his friend indulged in some manly gossip—of widower friends who had married for the second time, friends who got arrested for tax evasion, friends who had recently passed on. The guest kept throwing glances at me even when they were discussing people I did not know. Could this man be from an ad agency, the owner perhaps?

Then the conversation turned, to my surprise, to me. The guest asked me what I was doing, but his focus was mostly on my personal life, about my parents and my sibling. Now, why would a purported employer want to know all that?

When it was time for our usual walk, which I had thought would be shelved because of the presence of the visitor, Vik's dad said, "Let all go for a short walk. Brij and I take one every evening."

The guest gamely agreed, and we all set out. A cool evening breeze was blowing, and we retraced our usual route. The Gurkhas smiled at me and threw a salute at Vik's dad—he was that kind of a man, a commanding and prepossessing personality. An Alsatian here and a Doberman there barked with pleasure at seeing us, their old friends, again.

When we returned home, I was, as usual, out of breath. So was the guest for good measure. But not Vik's dad. The guest took leave at the gate, uttering the ominous sounding words, "See you all soon." He left in his silver-coloured Skoda.

Just before I went to bed, I heard the telephone downstairs ring insistently. Vik's dad took the call. After a brief conversation, he hung up.

The next morning before breakfast Vik's dad sent word through Rajamma that we needed to go out. I wanted to know more, but Rajamma said, "He didn't tell me where you were going."

I had a bath, got into some decent looking garments and came down. Vik's dad was ready and waiting. The car was already out of the garage and parked in the portico. A short-notice chauffeur was at hand.

"We are going to Dr. Chaudhury's clinic for a checkup and some tests," Vik's dad said, as if we were going to Moazzamjahi Market to do some shopping. "Dr. Chaudhury, whom you met yesterday, is a cardiologist."

Vik's dad couldn't have looked healthier. Puzzled, I enquired as we got into his Honda Accord: "Aren't you feeling well, Uncle?"

"You seem to have misunderstood. I apologize for springing this on you in this manner … The tests are for you, Brij. Dr. Chaudhury called me to ask if we could come today. He'll not be in town for the rest of the week."

"Why would I need any tests?"

"Dr. Chaudhury confirmed my suspicion that you could be suffering from a heart condition. He thinks it may be a congenital disorder. If the tests turn out to be positive, you may have to undergo a minor heart surgery."

"Heart surgery!" I almost had a heart attack then and there. "I don't have money for such fanciful things."

"Sorry, I didn't mean to startle you. Like I said the operation is going to be a minor one, if it is needed at all. And don't bother about the expenses; leave it to me. The important thing is that you must get well."

I sighed and looked out of the window. I did not know what to say. Or, for that matter, what to think. We were driving along the Hussain Sagar. In the distance I could see the immense granite Buddha in the middle of the lake. He had a forlorn expression, as if he was contemplating the unmitigated sadness of life.

In the context of nothing, I said, "I thought your friend was an owner of an ad agency! I had presumed the meeting was about a job for me."

"Not having a job shouldn't be your main worry, Brij. Health comes first. I have many friends in the advertising industry, and it will not be difficult to find you a position ..." He added with a smile, "Something that will give you pocket money."

For lack of anything to say, I said, "Thank you, Uncle."

"By the by, how is your idea for the ... er ... blog coming along?"

"Fine ... I want to call it 'Down and Out in Hyderabad'," I said, ad-libbing.

"What a pessimistic title! But yes, there are so many things to write about Hyderabad—whether good or bad. Once upon a time it was one of the cleanest and the most beautiful of cities. After all, the Sultan of Golconda had built it to rival Paradise."

"It's a lot closer to Hell right now," I said, as the car crouched in a traffic snarl under an infernal midmorning sun. A haze of dust and other pollutants hung like mist over the city.

"Perfect grist for your writer's mill. No doubt, life's full of challenges and disappointments. But there's one thing I've learned, Brij, even if a bit late in the day: in life, there's so much to be thankful for."

The Cost of Immigration

1: The Bookmark

The sliding glass doors rattled and shut behind Kamal as he stepped briskly out of the central library in Mississauga. He was a middle-aged man, short and stocky. A palpitating bundle of energy, he always moved about with a determined air even when he was attempting a most commonplace feat.

The crisp fall day had a rumour of chill in it. Nevertheless, Kamal decided to sit on one of the randomly placed, brightly coloured metal chairs—turquoise in this instance—to pore at leisure over the books he had borrowed. Tarrying for any reason was contrary to his inclination, but what the hell, this was his first free Saturday since he had given up his second job of many years. He wanted to savour to the fullest extent his newfound spare time. Even Katya, his wife, was always counselling him to go slow. Besides, in a couple of days he would turn fifty, and it was as good a time as any to reflect on life.

After placing the small pile of books on a round metal table, brightly painted in mandarin orange, Kamal looked around at the surroundings. Things had changed in so many ways in the ten years since he had arrived as an immigrant. Even more so in his own life, he thought with a sneaking sense of pride. He had been a lowly accountant in India having repeatedly failed to clear the certification exams related to his profession. When he couldn't climb the corporate ladder any further, despite having an uncanny ability to balance company books, he had taken recourse to immigration as an escape from a seemingly dead-end future.

Change was everywhere. A massive makeover had transformed the forecourt of the library. A large expanse of a tightly knit dark green lawn ended on one side with a performance stage, complete with ogle-eyed strobes, and speakers hanging like a Cubist version of gigantic birds' nests. On the other side, it reached the city hall rather indecisively—a splash pad in the summer, an ice-rink in the winter, and deserted in the fall.

Before the renovation, he remembered, there was a wooden statuary ring of paper-thin buffaloes in the centre of a humdrum patch of grass. He had often wondered as he hurried out of the library building (he was always rushing hither and thither in those early days) what the animals signified. Perhaps the buffaloes, which had been driven to near extinction, somehow symbolized the endangered species of genuine book readers, soon to become non-existent under the onslaught of electronic distractions.

A shrivelled maple leaf blew out of nowhere and landed at his feet. Like a business card from Mother Nature. In another few weeks, it would begin to snow, slowly bleeding the colours of the earth until the ground was nothing but white, and the sky a sombre grey.

Kamal had come wearing a T-shirt, not paying heed to Katya's advice to put on a fall jacket. How could you call yourself a Canadian, he had reasoned, if you're going to be fussy about the weather? Unmindful of the chill, he picked a book, and read the synopsis and the unreliable plaudits which were printed on the dust jacket. Apart from borrowing authors he liked, he had chosen—in an unacknowledged sexist way—books which would be of interest to Katya. Romances for her and thrillers and mysteries for himself.

As he gave the books a once-over, he found that one of them had a pasteboard card inserted inside to serve as an impromptu bookmark. It was an airline boarding card for a flight originating from India. He wanted to throw it away, but not finding a garbage bin close at hand he returned it to the book without a second glance.

Kamal sat there for a good half-hour, idle thoughts coasting by in his mind. Soon it was lunchtime, and he found people trickling out of the library building, some even braving the cold to eat lunch in the sun. The only food vendor, selling crêpes out of a cart, did not appear to attract any customers. Kamal always wondered what kind of money the man made. Canadians were a frugal lot, and more so the new immigrants who habitually hung around places like libraries and community centres. It looked as though the idle crêpe-seller, too, had come to sun himself in the square opposite the library building rather than to solicit customers.

Kamal recalled the days when he had worked in a grocery shop for the legislated minimum wage. The future had looked so bleak then, with no prospect of improvement in their financial situation. He'd been assailed by what can best be described as immigrant remorse: Had he jumped from the proverbial frying pan into the fire? His initial hopelessness had even communicated itself to Katya, who had been a homemaker her entire married life. A cool and composed woman, she too was spurred into action. But the resulting flurry of activity, which was little more than scattering her fluffed-up resume like a roadside evangelist distributing religious literature, had come to nothing. So, Kamal had hunted for a weekend job. While such employment seemed at first harder to find than a regular job, he was lucky to get a break as a security guard in a condo. From then on, he slogged every day of the week, taking no days off whatsoever except for an occasional three-week vacation to India to look up their parents. On her end, Katya held the domestic fort, and thanks to her, they didn't have to pay for daycare, and the children had someone to supervise them during the most critical period of their lives. Even after he had snagged a more lucrative job as an assembly-line worker, he retained his weekend job to pay the hefty mortgage for a detached home much larger than what was needed.

Their sacrifice had been well worth their while. His son, Nitin, after recently graduating as a computer engineer from the University of Toronto, had just joined a tech company in Ottawa. He was earning twice as much as his father had done working at two jobs. His daughter, Amita, was in Grade Twelve. She was six when they had come over and had a mind of her own even at that tender age. She was good at her studies, especially the sciences, and he hoped that she would become a doctor. Back home in India, generally parents wished that their sons become engineers and daughters, doctors. Like many an immigrant, he brought such aspirations into their new country of domicile, as if they were undeclared baggage.

When he looked back on the whole, he could say with confidence that his bold decision to immigrate to Canada was vindicated. In the first few years they'd been buffeted by many storms, some with forewarning, some without, but now the ship of life was progressing placidly on even keel. As an accountant he could certainly certify that the benefits of immigration had outweighed its costs.

When he returned home, he found that Katya was busy cooking. Good-humoured and comely (if one may use the old-fashioned word), she had retained much of her youthful prettiness, as though she had only matured, rather than aged, over time.

Katya never let Kamal into the kitchen, and he could never tell if it was because of kindness towards a person who worked two jobs or whether she thought him more of a nuisance than help. But one thing he could tell, from the aroma of strong spices which stampeded out of the kitchen, was that she was making Hyderabadi goat-biryani—his favourite dish.

A sudden thought popped into his mind: Did she get the date wrong? His fiftieth birthday was on the following Monday. He wanted to surprise them by taking the whole family (as Nitin, too, had agreed to nip down) to the restaurant high up in the CN Tower in downtown Toronto for dinner. The tower was one of the highest man-made structures in the world, and the restaurant had a 360-degree view of Toronto, at least, if not of the entire country or the planet itself. It was the right venue for the occasion—otherwise, too, he felt like he was on the top of the world.

He set the books on the table where their desolate landline telephone stood, idle as a museum piece. He switched on the TV, and sat down dutifully on the sofa opposite it, even though he knew of no show he wanted to watch at that hour.

"What books did you get for me?" Katya asked from the kitchen.

Before Kamal could turn down the volume and answer her, his daughter stormed into the room, talking incessantly into her phone. She had her father's aura of hyperactivity.

"Wait a moment, Ginny," she said, and then with an accusing tone addressed to her family, those present and absent, "I never find anything in this house!"

"What are you looking for?" Kamal said. "Can I help you?" he added unconvincingly. All these years he wasn't much around to be of any practical assistance to his children.

"Never mind, Dad ... I've found something."

His children had learned to cope without him. For all intents and purposes, he had become as irrelevant to them as the tabletop telephone instrument.

2: The Riddle

At around five in the evening, when he came down after a short and luxurious, but unaccustomed, siesta, piping hot masala chai was waiting for him. The perfect pick-me-up to ward off the late afternoon blues! Often Katya made light snacks to go with the tea, but today she seemed to be unaccountably occupied in the kitchen.

For lunch, he had expected to be served biryani, and when he remarked on its absence, his wife had retorted, "For a man who is so self-obsessed I'm surprised you noticed what was going on in the kitchen!"

Before he could rally his thoughts for a spirited defense (self-obsessed, indeed!) Katya offered an elaborate explanation: "Amita is having a potluck party at her friend's house in the evening. They're in the middle of some contest or campaign or something at her school. I believe it looks as if they are going to win the prize. They are having a review meeting, just to make sure they meet their target. But don't you worry, I've set aside some biryani for your dinner."

Kamal set down the empty mug with care on the marble coaster inlaid with fake gemstones, which they had picked up in India at a souvenir shop near the Taj Mahal. Katya, a house-proud person, hated to see rings left behind by mugs on the end tables. Also on the table was one of the books he had borrowed for Katya. There was a bookmark peeping out where Katya must have left off. She must have spent the afternoon reading when she found some respite from whatever she was preparing in the kitchen. He, too, had bravely tried reading the legal thriller he had borrowed for himself, but waves of drowsiness had lured him into taking a snooze.

The novel was a romantic thriller. Though he considered such books too sappy for his taste, the premise of the book was intriguing. It was about a young woman who commandeers a car under false pretences to undertake a trip to Delphi because she has no money. Quite an enterprising lass! He, too, had always harboured a desire to visit Greece. Images of the majestic Acropolis and the shimmering

Aegean islands flitted across his mind. While still in elementary school he had read about Greek heroes, demigods,
scientists, and philosophers. But when he lived in India, he
never had the money for foreign travel, and after he moved
to Canada, he never had the time.

He remembered with pleasure the novels he had read
by Eric Ambler and Alistair MacLean, which were set in
Greece, as he riffled the pages of the volume. The book fell
open on the page where the boarding card was stuck as a
bookmark. But this time round the reverse side of the
boarding card was visible. Squeezed into what little empty
space there was under the logo of the airline, an unknown
person had jotted something down. The handwriting was
unfamiliar. It was certainly not Katya's neat cursive, per-
fected in elementary school.

The penmanship was a hurried scrawl, and the enigmatic noting looked like a tally of some sort:

TPR	1,940
HR	800
GE	315
Al	405
GB	120
LP	156
TC	100
MT	?
	1,896

Always a sucker for a good conundrum, Kamal was intrigued
by the list. Was it made by the person who had taken the

transcontinental flight? Or by some random subsequent borrower of the library book?

One of Kamal's abiding interests while growing up in India was to devour the puzzles and pastimes page in the children's section of the *Deccan Chronicle*, the local English daily. Even after all these years, when he had a moment to spare, there was nothing he enjoyed more than a good crossword puzzle or a sudoku in the *Toronto Star*.

For good or for bad, his childhood interest had lingered into adulthood like a juvenile ailment—acne or a peanut allergy. At the get-togethers they held in their house, however few (thanks to his weekend job), Kamal always included a mind bender as a kind of a differentiator to make their parties unique. His guests, too, appeared to enjoy them—otherwise, wouldn't they have shunned his parties? In time, his quizzes had become as much a part of the menu as appetizers or dessert.

Kamal stared at the mysterious list for some time, trying to wring out some meaning. He sat there, not knowing for how long, his brain playing tug-o-war with the possibilities. Then at last, when he thought he saw a glimmer of a solution, he heard the doorbell ring. It took some time for him to detach himself from his present preoccupation and grope with his feet for his slippers. The doorbell pealed again, insistently, as though the ringer was running out of patience and was pouring out all his pent-up frustrations onto the electric bell.

Kamal rose, irritation furrowing his brow, and went to the front of the house wondering where on earth Katya and Amita were. They seemed to have deserted the house entirely in the period he was wrestling with the puzzle. When he threw open the door, he saw a host of people, anonymous for the initial split-second, but quickly morphing into a gallery of recognizable faces ... of his friends ... and even relatives. Katya and Amita, who must have let themselves out of the back door and gone around the house, were also there, grinning sheepishly. Both were dressed up for the party, Kamal noticed.

A deafening chorus of "Surprise!" broke like a monsoon thunderclap.

3. Celebration

"Happy Birthday!" his guests sang, trooping in: the Sharmas, the Raos, and the Kumars, not to mention his own family. Last to enter, smiling shamefacedly, was his son Nitin, flying in a day in advance. Nitin had the sweet and gentle aspect of his mother; and looking at odds was the big brown bag from the LCBO store tucked into the crook of his arm, making Kamal raise a quizzical eyebrow.

After handing over the gifts they had brought to a gobsmacked Kamal, the guests, who had come with their entire families in tow, seated themselves in the drawing room anywhere and everywhere—on sofas, on chairs, on armrests, and on the floor on cushions. They chattered and joked all at once, unable to believe what a thumping success their surprise had turned out to be.

Once the initial shellshock had evaporated, Kamal was left with a feeling of extreme shyness caused by his unceremonial attire—a faded T-shirt and pajamas. Soon, Nitin came over and compelled him to pop a magnum of Dom

Pérignon. Amita brought in a trayful of gleaming stemware of assorted sizes and shapes, most of them apparently borrowed beforehand from the households of the guests themselves. Katya produced, with the flair of a conjuror, a bottle of sparkling grape juice for the abstemious.

Sanjeev, one of his best friends, who had been an electrical engineer in India and was now a moderately successful real estate agent, raised a toast for Kamal. "For the golden boy, a loving husband, a responsible father, the best friend, and the most creative purveyor of party games! Three cheers!"

Another friend, Rajan, who had been a vet in India and now was eking out a living selling disability insurance, said, "Here's to the best dressed person in the place!"

Nitin re-entered the room carrying a huge slab of cake which seemed to have a wildfire raging on it. Fifty small candles blazed and smoked as the room exploded with merriment. While the guests cheered and clapped their hands, Kamal struggled to douse the conflagration with his breath.

One by one, Kamal's friends came up to shake hands with him. Katya kissed him demurely on his cheek; his children hugged him. When Kamal requested a few minutes to change his clothes, Rajan said, "You're not going anywhere, man. You look great as you are!"

"Aren't we going to have a quiz game?" Atul asked. He was a bright twelve-year-old boy who attended a special school for gifted children.

"Kamal-uncle didn't know about the party, so he didn't have time to prepare one," Katya said.

The boy turned to the crowd, grinned, and said, pumping his arm, "Yippee!"

"Not so fast, young man," Kamal said. "I may not have had the time to make up a quiz, but I do have something up my sleeve. Give me a moment."

He pulled out the boarding card he had found inserted in Katya's novel and disappeared into the spare bedroom on the ground floor which doubled as a study. After a few minutes, Kamal emerged from the den carrying a sheaf of photocopies. The party noises began to ebb like water gurgling down a drain. But Amita's mobile, which refused to lie dormant for more than a few minutes at a time, trilled penetratingly again. Amita left the room, saying into her phone, "I can't hear you, Maryanne. There's too much noise here ..."

In the ensuing silence, Kamal distributed the sheets among his curious guests. Waving the original boarding card, Kamal said, "I found this in a library book. Somebody had used it as a bookmark. At first, I didn't think much of it. As you all can see, it was just a boarding pass for a flight from India to Canada. But later when I turned it over, I found that somebody had scribbled a list of some sort. I tried to figure out what it meant. It took me some time to work it out. In fact, the answer was just dawning on me when you all created that ruckus with the doorbell. But now it's your turn to put on your thinking caps. Let's see what you'll come up with."

"What kind of a quiz is this?" Atul asked, staring at the Xeroxed sheet with some disappointment. "It looks like my Chennai granny's laundry list."

"Look at the numbers, boy," Kamal said. "Your grandmother must have a whole lot of dirty linen to wash!"

Some of the guests pored over it while others gave it only a cursory glance, but the party progressed with the usual verve and bonhomie. Katya brought in tray after tray of finger foods—Indian stuff, like mini-samosas and minced-meat vadas, along with outlandish snacks like bruschetta and spring rolls. Kamal never suspected she could make the latter kind of stuff. In life, Kamal had been content to eat her dal and vegetable curry with boiled rice, with fish or chicken on occasion and, except for a yearning for biryani, had sought no more. Most importantly, where did she find the time to make so many dishes? How did she so success-fully hide her efforts from him, aside from the one clue of the irrepressible fragrance of Hyderabadi biryani permeat-ing out of the kitchen?

"... Could it be a grocery list?" Prabhakar said.

"It must be a very big family with a very big appetite!" Kamal said.

"An annual list, perhaps?"

Kamal shook his head. "Whoever does that now—buy-ing in bulk for the entire year?"

Sanjeev looked up from the sheet of paper he was avidly gazing at and said, "Is it a list of stock market trades?"

"Interesting. What makes you think so?"

"There's an entry, GE. Perhaps it stands for General Electric? HR for Healthcare Realty?"

"Excellent try, but sorry I don't think it's so. The num-bers on the list don't look like their stock prices to me."

The younger guests seemed to get bored of the game and began to talk and laugh among themselves in hushed tones. Soon they moved almost *en masse* to another part of the house for more freedom.

Sujatha, his friend Lalit's wife said, "Is it a list of dona-tions for a social cause?"

"Hmm ... well, it could be, but it's too general an explanation. I'm looking for something more specific."

Soon they broke for dinner, the guests gladly suspending their speculation about the bookmark. After they finished dinner, a sumptuous spread clandestinely prepared by Katya, which featured not only her incomparable Hyderabadi biryani, but also the usual suspects like butter chicken, vegetable korma, naan, and raita, the guests reconvened in the living room. While tucking into ras malai, the oversweet dessert made with casein, milk and sugar, they listened to Kamal giving his take on the bookmark puzzle.

4. An Imaginary Life

Kamal picked up the boarding pass and, after clearing his throat, said, "People take a bookmark for granted even it's beautifully made let alone an improvised one like this one. Even I, when I first came upon it, wanted to consign it to a trash can. Bookmarks seemingly have a limited function. It's just a place holder for the period starting from when you've discontinued reading a book and to when you returned to it later.

"But only when we pause to think about a bookmark's life will we discover how unique it is. It spends all its active life in the company of books. And in such intimacy, too, locked as it were in a book's bear hug. Is it any wonder, then, if a bookmark is privy to countless stories, stories crafted by a variety of authors, in genres of every kind? If they had tongues how many fascinating tales they could retell!

"This oblong piece of pasteboard, which was transformed into an improvised bookmark by a lazy reader, has a story to tell too. A saga not imagined by the author of the book, but a chapter of life unintentionally left behind perhaps by one of its readers ...

"I think this is what happened ..." Reading the name from the back of the boarding pass, "Tiwari ... came to Canada in the spring of this year along with his wife and two young children."

"How would you know that, Sherlock?" Sanjeev said.

"I'm only guessing ..." Kamal said. "The seat number 52E. He must have had all four seats in the central section. If they were only two or three of them, he would have got the seats abutting the window. If he was alone, he would have opted for a window seat or an aisle. As they were immigrating, he would have booked early and would have had the pick of the seats. His seat number is considered the better one in a large aircraft used for transcontinental flights.

"The family landed at Toronto's Pearson airport, their eyes lighting up with hope and excitement. Initially, everything went swimmingly. It was a breeze to admit your children into a good neighbourhood school—unlike back home where you run from pillar to post. It was just as easy to apply for a Social Insurance card, and the Ontario Health card, though you had to wait out a three-month cooling period, hoping nothing untoward happened to you and your family in the meanwhile. They enrolled in the library; how bright and spacious it was, overflowing with books, videos, DVDs, and computer facilities to conduct your job search.

"Even to buy a car seemed a piece of cake. Here anybody could afford a car, it appeared. It was only later they came to know of the steep auto insurance cost. It was not long before they encountered their first reality check: employment in a field which you were qualified and trained for was impossible to get.

"Arjun couldn't find work commensurate with his education and experience. His wife, for some reason, didn't or couldn't find suitable employment either. In desperation, Arjun settled for a survival job as a security guard or a warehouse worker. The new job which fetched slightly more than the minimum wage seemed to staunch their expenses, but was it enough?

"Arjun decided to put down their monthly expenses on a whim. Not finding a notepad or something suitable in the drawer of their dresser, he must have chanced upon the old boarding cards stowed there along with their Indian passports and other travel documents. Without further ado, he quickly jotted down the monthly expenses on the card."

"Kamal, why would anyone retain old boarding cards?" Sanjeev asked.

"For sentimental reasons, perhaps?" Mridula, Rajan's wife, said. "Immigration is a big step in one's life. We also saved those boarding cards. In fact, they are still around in some drawer or cupboard."

"Are you sure, dear," his Katya asked, "that it was your imaginary immigrant who scribbled those figures? If you ask me ..."

Gesturing to Katya to pipe down, Kamal said, "Reasonably sure, my dear. Going by the Sherlockian adage, 'Once you eliminate the impossible, whatever remains, no matter how improbable, must be the truth.' Anyway, to continue, this is what the initials stand for:

Total Pay Received	1,940
House Rent	800
Grocery Expenses	315
Automobile Insurance	405
Gas Bill	120
Loan Payments	156
Telephone, Cable	100
Miscellaneous Things	?
	1,896

"As you can see his earnings were barely covering his monthly expenses. He was in a real quandary. This couldn't go on. Expenses tend to mount over time, but earnings go up only marginally, at least in Canada. They had to think up of something to save the situation."

"It sounds so much like my situation in the first few months after we arrived in Canada," Prabhakar said.

"It's pretty much every new immigrant's story I guess," Rajan said.

"How do you think it ended for this man?" Sujatha asked. "The important lesson one learns after immigrating is about the value of persevering. Things may seem extremely challenging in the first few years, but afterwards everything falls into place, and life begins to look up."

"Hopefully, he found a job which paid better," Sanjeev said.

"Small chance of that," Rajan said with a wry chuckle.

"Perhaps his wife got herself a job—in Tim Hortons or McDonald's. The pay may not be much but every bit helps," Mridula said, who worked as a shop assistant.

"Or, he must have looked for a weekend job to supplement his income," Kamal said in a low voice.

"If I were him, I would return to India double quick," Prabhakar said, one of the lucky few who had got a reasonably good job in a not-for-profit organization no sooner than he landed in Canada.

A contemplative silence settled over the room while the adults present reminisced about their not-so-distant past. How often in those first few years, when everything seemed so discouraging, they had to steel themselves and persevere rather than yield to the temptation to throw in the towel. For each one of them, it was like replaying their personal montage of hopes and fears, both equally unrealistic, which had been archived in a remote vault of their memory.

The brief spell of silence was broken by Atul. "I think Uncle's explanation is a lot of bull!" He had not left the room with the other children, not being enamoured of their juvenile pursuits.

"Shh!" his mother said. "You don't speak to elders like that!"

"Allow him to speak," Katya said. "Why do you say that, Atul?"

"Uncle said that GB stands for Gas Bill. When we were new to Canada, Daddy always called gas 'petrol'. If the man had just arrived in Canada, he would have written PB."

"A good point, I concede," Kamal said. "But some people are quicker than others to learn the local lingo."

Just then Amita entered the room, with her mobile glued to her ear, as if the organ would fall off were it not held in its place by the telephone instrument. Amita had been making entrances and exits all through the evening to the dictates of her mobile. She was talking with serious intent into the mouthpiece, as she headed straight to the telephone table. She started moving things about with growing impatience.

"I never find anything in this house! I left some important notes on this table in the afternoon. Did either of you touch it?" Amita said, looking accusatorially at her mother and father, with the filial impatience of the modern generation.

Then her eyes narrowed. She strode purposefully to her father and snatched the boarding card from his hand.

"What are you doing with it?" she asked imperiously. "I jotted down the individual score of our team members."

"Is this list made by you?" a startled Kamal asked.

"Couldn't you recognize my handwriting?" Amita said.

"I could have told you, Kamal, if you had only bothered to listen," Katya said. "I had realized the list must be something to do with the contest they are having in their school."

"Yeah," Amita said. "It's a list of individual points earned by my team members. The initials are of my teammates."

"Oh!" was all Kamal could muster.

"Hey Amita, what does TPR stand for?" asked Nitin.

"Total Points Required. It's the number we have to beat to win."

"That's a real anti-climax," Sanjeev said, with a laugh which was almost a snigger.

"But it was a nice story," Sujata said. "Sometimes it is good to be reminded of our past lest we become complacent."

"It was quite poignant. Close to the bone—even though it turned out to be pure fiction in the end," Mridula said. There was a film of tears in her eyes.

"Yo, Amita," Atul said. "What does AI stand for? Not Automobile Insurance, surely?"

"AI stands for Always Impertinent," Nitin said. "Hey, Dad! In all this excitement, I forgot something ... I brought you a gift." Nitin delved his right hand into his inside jacket pocket, pulled out a longish envelope and proffered it to his father.

"To the best dad in the world! And I really mean it," Nitin said, hugging Kamal. A quiet Kamal took the envelope and tore it open. Inside were travel vouchers, including boarding passes, for a cruise in the Aegean for all four members of the Shantaram family.

Finding Kitty

Rathi had sent her family into a tizzy again.

The interview for her very first job after she and her parents moved back to India was in another hour and a half. A regular job, nine to five and all that. Not the cafeteria-help kind of stints she had been used to as a student in Canada.

And as usual everything was falling to pieces. Her professional-looking black leather binder, for no real reason, had sprung a tear at the spine, and Daddy was insisting that she take all her original certificates with her, and when she had objected—"Rats, because that's how it is done in India!"

Her classmates in Canada had trimmed her name— short as it was—with an unconscious desire to impart a familiar twist to a foreign sounding moniker. Daddy had taken an inexplicable liking to the diminutive, and often used it at home. Mummy, a no-nonsense person, had felt no such urge to live up to the junior joneses.

Daddy was already agitated. The mechanic who had promised to repair their car overnight and bring it in time the next morning was untraceable. The mobile constantly crooned a jaunty Bollywood number, its owner having blithely gone AWOL.

Mummy was in a bind too. The drinking water pipes were bone dry. They were supposed to be operational from six to eight in the morning. Today, as Mummy had said, of all days! The tap was resolutely silent but for blowing an eerie whistle or two every now and then.

"This is India," Dad had said, with an oracular gravity. "We must never lose sight of it."

Fat lot of chance there was of overlooking the vast country anyways. Not half as large as Canada, but with nearly fifty times its population. And the moment you stepped out, the smells, the noise, let alone the sights, simply overpowered you. It was so different from the atmosphere Rats was used to for the past fifteen years: the unchallenged quiet of Canadian suburbia, its deserted byways where only an occasional car would appear, and the lonely sidewalks with hardly any pedestrians except for a rare dog-walker or a jogger.

"The car won't be here in time," Daddy said. "You will have to take an autorickshaw to the interview. I can accompany you if you like."

"I can manage, Daddy," Rats said, mussing Puddles' head. Puddles was an Irish terrier, the last of a long line of pets she has had since she was four. He had not taken so badly to immigrating to India, but he wisely preferred to spend time only in the air-conditioned parts of the house.

"Rathi, I don't think it's wise to go on your own," Mummy said.

"Nothing's going to happen to me in broad daylight!"

"No, I was thinking of the language barrier. You don't get what locals are trying to say, and they in turn don't understand your hybrid Telugu."

"It's not so bad, Mummy. I'm improving, and how will I learn if I don't try?"

"Well, don't say I didn't warn you if the autorickshaw takes you to a wrong address."

"It was same thing when we first went to Canada," Daddy said. "We couldn't follow their Canadian accent, and they couldn't understand our Indian English ... But Rats, remember to take your mobile with you. And don't forget to buy a new binder at the stationery shop on the main road. The quality of the binder may not be good, so make sure it's at least presentable. It needs to last only for a day, we can buy a good quality leather one later."

"All the best for the interview," Mummy said, coming to the front door. "Don't be too nervous."

Rats walked down the lane which led to the main road. Emaciated trees, ringed with robust metal guards, lined the road. The sidewalk, uneven here and there, was reasonably clean, having been swept early in the morning, but there were indelible splashes of betel-stained spittle, like a trail of blood stains in a CSI TV show. Pasted on the compound walls of houses were collages of handbills and posters, advertising kindergarten schools, political public meetings, and such.

At the Sri Rama Stationery and General Store, Rats chose an uninspiring maroon binder, the only sober looking one, the other options being lemon yellow, sky blue and blood red. The binder was flimsy, as Daddy had predicted, but it would do for now. While still in the shop, she tried to transfer her stuff from the old binder into the new one. She was clumsy, dropping the documents on to the floor more than once. Had her nervousness already kicked in?

The shopkeeper, far from being disapproving, volunteered to help her. He forcibly took the binders from her and neatly and quickly effected the change, inserting the documents in the right chronological order.

"Best of luck for your interview," he said as if clairvoyant.

Rats stepped out of the shop and looked for an autorickshaw. A little farther down the road, she saw two empty ones pulled up along the sidewalk back-to-back. Painted an unseemly yellow, they looked like a pair of jaundiced baby elephants. She walked up and enquired of the first autorickshaw. When she gave out her destination, the driver shook his head and told her unenthusiastically that he didn't intend to head in that direction. Then Rats moved on to the next one, whose driver was curled up in the passenger seat at the back, smoking a beedi, the local version of a cigarillo. When Rats asked of him, he lazily pointed at the fare meter. It was draped with his khaki uniform-coat. It dawned on Rats that a shrouded meter supposedly meant the autorickshaw was not in service.

She looked about with rising anxiety wondering if she would be able to make it to the interview in time. Luckily, she spotted an autorickshaw on the other side of the road. She waited for some time at the traffic signals before realizing that the go light for pedestrians, the white walking man, was never going to appear. He must have been kidnapped and put away by the powerful lobby of vehicle owners. She would have to cross the road like everybody else—the devil-may-care jaywalkers.

It was then that she saw the woman at the street corner. She was wearing an unpressed sari which made her look stodgy. She wore, as Rats was learning to notice, minimal but mandatory gold jewellery on her: thin gold bangles, small gold earrings, and a simple gold chain bearing the thaali—the symbol of wifehood. The woman was middle-aged, and her hair was beginning to grey. Her face looked careworn.

Rats thought, "A kindred spirit! She's also nervous about crossing roads."

The woman looked at her and said something. Her lips formed illegible words, and the air failed to carry the sounds over the tumult of the traffic. But her eyes looked entreatingly at Rats.

Rats approached the lady, and said, "Yes?"

"Have you seen my kitty?" the woman asked. "I've lost my kitty!"

"No," Rats said, scanning the busy intersection around her for the purportedly missing kitten. "Did it run away from you? It will come back, I'm sure. They always do."

"I have been waiting for a long time," the woman said forlornly. "Please help me in finding my kitty," the woman said, who herself looked lost.

"Please wait here," Rats said, "while I go and look around."

Rats went up the side street looking for the kitten. Even the side road was busy, with the noise of moving people, animals, and machines. A cow, yes, a pi-dog, yes, but a kitten? No. It could be anywhere, hiding in any nook and corner of this warren—frightened and whimpering. Or maybe not. Cats were agile and resilient. They were survivors.

Rats spent a good ten minutes scouring the lanes and bylanes and then she went back to the woman. She was still at the street corner, raking the landscape with her eyes.

"You know, animals are more intelligent than we think," Rats said, her Telugu peppered with English words. "It must have gone back home by now. Why don't you go home and check?"

The woman shook her head emphatically. "Kitty got lost here. He will not be at home."

"I'll tell you what. I'll take you home. My bet is you'll find your kitty there."

"You don't have to take me home. I can manage. I live nearby," the woman said as if digging her heels in.

Rats took the woman's hand, and tugging it, she said, "It's getting to be too hot now. Let's go." Rats could already feel sweat and heat on her skin, like being licked wetly by a passionate sun.

The woman complied, and led by her, they entered a small lane off the main road. Along the way, the big, brightly lit shops yielded to smaller businesses like tailors, tea shops, and motorcycle mechanics. Then, the residential quarters took over from commercial establishments. Some of the houses were of modest size, with their own tiny courtyards. Some were so small that their front doors opened right onto the pavement, and each had a long string of alpha-numeric door numbers, with many slashes and dashes, prominently painted on the front doors. The woman's house was set in a small compound, and its forecourt had

sacred basil growing in an ornamental urn. In whatever
little space was available around the house, a few flowering
shrubs like jasmine and roses—desperately in need of fertilizer—were planted.

"Would you like to come in and have some coffee?" the
woman asked.

"No, I must get going. I have a job interview to attend."

"Let's meet again," the woman said perfunctorily, using
the Telugu phrase for goodbye without literally meaning it.

On her way back to the main road, Rats found a daw-
dling autorickshaw on the lookout for a customer. Rats
hailed it, and mercifully this time round the driver had
nothing to quibble about.

* * *

The venue of the job interview was a pricey hotel. The lobby
was busy with the traffic of guests coming in, going out, or
just standing around the front desk. A breathless bellhop
was skittering all over the place, following the bidding of all
and sundry at the same time.

On an easel in a corner was a black message board with
white detachable letters which directed the interviewees to
the conference hall downstairs. Rats descended the wide
sweeping circular staircase which led to a netherworld
steeped in chandeliered luxury. Though there were many
candidates seated in the foyer of the conference hall, a remarkable silence prevailed. All the circumspectly seated
candidates had folders, containing their precious educa-
tional certificates, placed on their laps. With good reason
they clung to their folders with both hands. In a country

of more than a billion people, education alone was the passport for a lucrative job, especially for those without "connections."

At the far end was a large table presided over by a young woman. Dressed in a chic silk sari, she was good-looking, and exuded confidence. But boredom was already stealing over her. She camouflaged a yawn with one palm, even as she attempted either a crossword or a sudoku in a newspaper with the other. Rats approached the lady with an expression she hoped was penitential and introduced herself.

"You are very late! You've missed your turn," she said in a tone which implied that was that and nothing could be done.

"I'm sorry! I ... I ..."

"Aha, you are the Canadian girl!" she said, as she consulted a list of names. Then she asked drily, "Were you also caught in a traffic jam?"

"No ... I ... I ..."

"Say no more! That's good enough," she said, with a small smile burgeoning on her subtly painted corporate lips. "I'm not going to ask you for the reason. Boy, am I not tired of unpunctual candidates telling me they got stuck in the traffic!"

"Thank you," Rats said, relief washing over her. She would never have succeeded in explaining herself articulately. Besides, what would a right-minded hirer think of a candidate who goes off on wild cat missions unmindful of an upcoming job interview?

"You will have to wait until all the candidates who have come on time, some in fact *much* before, finish their interviews. It could well be the end of the day by then."

"Oh!"

"Don't look so alarmed. I was just joking. If I find a vacant slot, I'll fit you in. But whatever your excuse for coming in late, it'd better be good. Mr. Kameshwar *absolutely* abhors tardiness."

Rats walked away from the reception table and found a secluded corner from where she called home to tell her parents about the delay and the reason for it. The only comment from Mummy was, "Really!"

Rats joined the solemn congregation in the waiting area to bide her time. She had been forewarned by Daddy long ago, that to survive in India one must have enormous patience. Nothing ever happened on time. But this time round the delay was of her own making, and she girded herself for a long wait.

There were newspapers on end tables, but Rats had not got into the routine of reading Indian papers. They, like everything else in the country, presented a riotous melange. And there was an overdose of abbreviations, all meaningless to Rats, sprinkled like garnish over actual news.

At about two-thirty in the afternoon, when butterflies and hunger had almost gnawed her innards to tatters, the young woman bade her into the holy of holies.

"Your lucky day! Another no-show," the young woman said. "Caught in a traffic snarl, no doubt."

The temperature inside the room was a few degrees lower than the rest of the hotel, which itself had felt polar. Mr. Kameshwar greeted her with a smile which was beginning to fray at the edges from constant use. He appeared like all well-to-do in India: sleek hair groomed with hair oil, a lounge suit made by an expert bespoke tailor, an eye-catching silk tie, a pair of gold cufflinks, and the merest suggestion of expensive cologne.

Mr. Kameshwar picked up a two-page document from a stack on the table. Rathi recognized it as the biodata she had composed with massive input from Daddy. After a brief glance at her resume, he looked up and asked her, "When you returned, what were your first impressions of India?"

Rats was relieved that the first question was not about her coming late for the interview. She took some time to collect her thoughts before giving tongue to her opinion: the crowds, the colours, the noise, the heat, the dust, the smells, the dirt. She hoped she did not sound too much like a stereotypical tourist from the West.

"... But the people here are warm and generous," she said tamely, just in case her honest first impressions had offended him.

Mr. Kameshwar gave her a knowing smile, and said, "If you could describe India in a phrase, what would it be?"

Rats began to think furiously, even though the question seemed a bit too profound for the occasion. Mr. Kameshwar, perhaps having realized his folly, hastily added, "If you can't think up of an answer it's OK. It was not fair on my part to ask you that question in the first place."

From the tempestuous welter of thoughts in her mind, her very own definition of India spilled out. "Orderly chaos." That was how she had felt; everything appeared messy at the surface, but deep down somewhere was a vein of ancient wisdom.

"Nicely put," Mr. Kameshwar said, "even if a bit contradictory. I always felt the phrase 'Modern India' itself is an oxymoron."

When Mr. Kameshwar enquired about her many, if too brief, forays into the labour market, she narrated her experiences, not knowing how they would be interpreted. Of the mischievous twins who couldn't, or simply wouldn't, get a grip on algebra when she gave private tuition. Of how her mom shadowed her like a determined stalker when she was delivering the *Mississauga News* from door to door. Of the many challenges of working in campus coffee shops. Mr. Kameshwar seemed more amused than interested.

But to a pointed question on customer service, she had to admit, "The most difficulty I had was in understanding the orders of South Indians because of their accent. Though I am a South Indian myself."

"So am I. But you are doing quite well, I must say."

Then he continued to speak, with uncommon warmth in his voice, of his company which was family-owned for generations. It was into the manufacture and sale of a variety of products such as pickles, toilet soaps, hair oil, and alarm clocks. But lately, they had perceived an urgent need to adapt to a rapidly changing world.

"After many deliberations, we have decided to go into products using new technologies. We are now focussing on alternate energy for household use. We are starting small, that's why we have advertised for only twenty sales positions. But can you imagine how many applications we received?"

Rats shook her head.

"Five thousand!"

"Wow! But on second thought, I'm not surprised."

"Though we have a large pool of talent to pick from, it's as much a challenge to choose the right kind of personnel, individuals who will be in step with our corporate culture. Many young Indians may lack soft skills, but they are quick learners, and we can groom them. We are looking for people with fire in their belly."

Rats was silent. The implication was clear: she may not have what it takes to do the job. Mr. Kameshwar looked at his watch. The interview is over, Rats thought.

"By the way," Mr. Kameshwar said, abruptly changing the tenor of his talk, "what made you come late for the interview?"

A momentary silence followed the question which had until then remained unspoken, hanging over the interview like a dark monsoon cloud. Taking a deep breath, like how one does before diving off a very high board in a community pool, Rats took the plunge. She narrated her escapade, feeling like a total loser. What corporate house worth its salt would like its employee to get lured away from her objective? Besides, she had not even been successful. Daddy always told her that in business, or for that matter in any department of life, nothing succeeds like success.

Mr. Kameshwar's response came as a surprise to Rats. "That was a very selfless act. You don't see that kind of empathy in youth nowadays."

Rats muttered an almost inaudible thank-you.

"Are you fond of animals?" Mr. Kameshwar said.

A bouquet of thoughts burst in her mind: the succession of pets she had had, a hamster named Hamburger, a pair of parakeets called Bonnie and Clyde, and, last but not least, Puddles. But even before Rats could put together a cogent answer, Mr. Kameshwar, without waiting for her response, pressed on, "One of my cousins, who is also a director in our company, runs a shelter for stray and abandoned animals. Of course, most of the people working there are volunteers, but there are a few paid staff too. The charity mostly gets by with corporate and private donations. I'm told running such an enterprise is a more daunting task than managing a conventional business enterprise."

"I'm sure," said Rats, just to contribute to the conversation.

Mr. Kameshwar looked at his wristwatch—solid gold or gold-plated at the very least—and said, "Well, thank you for your time, Rathi. We'll let you know of our decision soon."

* * *

More than a fortnight passed but there was no news from the company. Just when she thought her job interview was a lost cause, she received a call from the animal shelter run by Mr. Kameshwar's cousin. Would she be interested in joining them? Of course, the salary would not be great shakes, but perhaps she would find the work rewarding?

She had a week to decide. Her parents were more than encouraging, in fact they interpreted the job offer as a sign of evolving India, where people aspired to be something other than doctors or engineers, where paid work was available not just in banks and businesses.

Once she took the job, Rats commuted to work like everybody else, using public transit or a shared autorickshaw. It was while riding a shared autorickshaw one morning that she spotted the woman at the street corner again. The woman, as was her wont, was anxiously casing the landscape, waiting for her beloved pet to materialize.

Rats could not stop the autorickshaw, however much she wanted to, as she was in the company of two strangers. But when she reached her place of work, an idea took shape in her mind.

A little before noon on the same day, she spoke to the head of the animal shelter.

"Of course," the president said. "If it is a good and caring family, we have no objections at all."

That afternoon, Rats left work early. She couldn't take either public transit or a shared autorickshaw as neither of her hands was free. Carrying her handbag, the lunch box, and her precious cargo, she got into a regular autorickshaw. Less expensive than a taxi, it would still cost the earth.

When she got off at the crossroads, the familiar figure was missing from the scene. Rats was a little disappointed. In her mind, the woman had become as good as a piece of street furniture. But since she knew where the woman lived, she took the bylane which led to her house. It took longer than she expected to reach the house with the small courtyard and scanty garden.

Rats knocked on the door with her knuckles as there was no electric bell. She heard shuffling feet before the door was flung open.

"Yes?" a young woman said, her hand on the inside door handle, ready to slam shut at any hint of trouble.

"I'm Rathi," Rats said, words stumbling out. "I've come to meet the woman ... the woman who often stands at the crossroads ..."

A look of puzzlement came over the young woman's face. Obviously, somebody who dressed and spoke like Rats

would not normally turn up at her doorstep. Unless she had
lost her way.

"I'm her friend. I've brought something for her."

The puzzlement on her face grew deeper when she
noticed what Rats was carrying in her hands.

She turned her head and said over her shoulder
"Sarojamma, somebody has come to meet you." Switching
on a hospitable smile, she said to Rats, "My aunt will be
here in a moment. Please come in."

It was dark inside, but Rats could make out the general
layout from the little light that infiltrated the room. The
window must have been kept deliberately closed to keep out
the dust from the abutting road. There was a lingering
smell of joss ticks and unseen drains.

"Where are you from?" the young woman asked matter-
of-factly, as she put on a ceiling light. That perennial question again! No matter how much Rats tried to integrate
herself, the local people at once took her to be an outsider.

"I *am* from Hyderabad, but we lived in Canada for
many years."

"Oh. Is it in America?" She was not exactly right, but
Rats was not inclined to correct her.

Her friend manqué, the woman at the crossroads, came
into living room. She looked at Rats uncomprehendingly at
first, then a small shy smile of recognition replaced her
habitually melancholic expression.

"I didn't find you at the usual place, so I took the lib-
erty of coming to your house."

"I'm glad you did. Please, why don't you take a seat?
Would you like to have a cup of tea?"

"I'm fine. I have brought a present for you," Rats said, handing over the small kitten she had brought along with her from the shelter.

The kitten mewled as it left the comfort of Rat's arms for Sarojamma's reluctant grasp. The look of incomprehension returned to Sarojamma's face.

"It looks like your pet cat is lost forever, so I have brought another one for you," said Rats.

"What pet cat?" the young woman asked. Sarojamma was holding the kitten as if it were a dripping octopus.

"Kitty. The one she's searching for at the crossroads every day."

"Kitti's not a cat. Kitti was her son Kirtan's pet name. Years ago, the boy went missing ... One afternoon, the two of them were taking a stroll on the main road when the little boy wandered away. Sarojamma was busy looking at the wares in the shop windows and did not realise that Kitti was not with her. But when she did, he was nowhere to be found. She ran up and down the road like a demented woman, but she never found him."

"How could a boy disappear like that from the main road with so many people around?" Rats asked.

"We don't know," the young woman said. "We made a police complaint but nothing came out of it. Somebody must have found Kitti all alone and whisked him away. It could have been someone from a beggars' gang, or somebody who saw the chance to sell him to a family wanting a male heir. You know how crazy some parents are to have a male child."

"Yes, I've heard about it."

"Sarojamma was never the same after that. She still thinks her son will return one day. That's why she goes to the crossroads every day, hoping to meet him when he returns."

"I'm sorry. I think I've made a ghastly mistake. I have misunderstood the entire situation ..." Rats faltered, feeling confused and contrite at the same time.

"You don't have to feel apologetic. You are a very kind person. Few people in this world will go to so much trouble to help an unhappy fellow human being."

"Thank you. That makes me feel better," said Rats. "But I don't want to force the kitten on Sarojamma. I'm prepared to take it back—"

"There's no need to do that. Look!"

The kitten, which had stopped whining, had made itself at home in the crook of the Sarojamma's arm. Hugging the kitten, Sarojamma was gently stroking it, as a mother does to soothe a colicky baby.

When it was time for Rats to leave, Sarojamma said, with an expression as contented as it was rare, "Let's meet again."

The Lime Tree

It was only a coarse brown envelope from home, but it fetched a smile of pleasure in me. I had been feeling low, facing an uncertain future as an international student studying in Toronto. The latest changes to immigration laws had made returning to India a real possibility.

I knew what the package would contain: a copy of my sister's first book of poetry. She was in her early twenties like me but was already being noticed as a social activist and a writer. I was flipping through the slim volume when a poem's title made me stop. I started to read:

> *A tree so beautiful*
> *Like nothing on this earth!*
> *It could've only been transplanted*
> *From some celestial arbour*

As I was reading, memories jostled their way into my mind ...

* * *

You can see the tree when you round the last corner on the
way to Grandma's house. The tree grows in her neighbour's
lot. But we aren't looking. I'm busy with a game on my phone;
my sister Mithuna has her head turned away, gazing at the
hillside to our right; Aunty's in the middle of her customary
joust with the taxi-driver about the extortionate fare.

Aunty is Daddy's second or third cousin. For the last two
years, she's been chaperoning us on holidays while our parents are tied up with their fledgling consultancy business.

The taxi comes to a stop in front of Grandma's house.
The driver toots, *pom, pom, pom-pom-pom!* As we step out,
Aunty emits a loud gasp. Thinking Aunty's being strangled
by the irate driver I turn my head with interest. But Aunty's
staring in the direction of our neighbour's compound. Then
I, too, notice the object which has triggered her amazement.

> *Resplendent in a garment verdant*
> *Bedecked with fruit that shine*
> *In the clear morning light—*
> *Like jewels rarely seen*

It's the same lime tree which had looked so emaciated
last year that it made Mithuna joke that it was suffering
from scurvy.

Grandma comes to the front door, beaming. Close on
her heels is the new maidservant, Nirmala, also beaming,
presumably catching the contagion from my grandma since
she has never seen us before. Grandma hugs Mithuna and
me, enveloping us with the smells of old age and the day's
cooking. I'm surprised to notice how much she seems to
have shrunk. I remember her as a strong, tall woman. But
then, I've put on nearly a foot since we last saw her.

"Smile, child," she says to my sister. Mithuna had been difficult throughout the journey—sometimes overexcited, sometimes morose, but always managing to annoy Aunty. And Grandma says to me, "How tall you've grown!"

I avoid my sister's eye. We're twins. I'm older by a few minutes, but we look so different from each other that nobody would take us for siblings even. We're fifteen years of age. I'm fair of skin, tall and strong for my age. On my cheeks, there's already a shadowy presence of facial hair. I love sports and play soccer and tennis. I'm good at studies, too, especially math.

My sister's small-built, almost scrawny, and looks more of a child than a teenager. She's coffee-bean brown, taking after my father. In a colour-conscious country like India, her dark complexion is deplored by aunts and grandaunts who see a dim future for her in the marriage market.

And while my twin's no great shakes when it comes to schoolwork, she reads a lot and occasionally writes poetry.

Grandma's house is not large. It has three or four rooms, apart from a kitchen and a bathroom. It's surrounded by tall, leafy trees, and the old tiled roof is apt to leak when it rains hard. It's dark inside, memories and secrets lurk in its nooks and corners.

I'm the first to go to the bathroom, a small box of a room with a cement floor and only one tap. For hot water you've got to dip into a large urn which is heated by burning firewood in an opening on the outer wall.

After all of us have bathed, we sit down cross-legged on mats in the kitchen for lunch. It's uncomfortable, but how delicious the simple meal tastes—piping hot, made from fresh ground spices and vegetables picked the same morning from the kitchen garden at the back of the house.

"Unless you eat, how will you grow tall?" my grandmother says to Mithuna, who had refused a second helping.

"Mithuna's always picky about food. In fact, she's fussy
about everything!" Aunty says with a snort.

"Leave her alone, Aunty" I say. "You know she's still
quite upset."

"Are you thinking about what happened last year, love?"
Grandma says to Mithuna. "You must learn to let go, dear."

Mithuna purses her lips. There's an awkward pause for
few moments.

"The pickle is so fresh and delicious!" Aunty says,
prompting Grandma to give her another dollop of the pickle
made of wedges of sunshine-yellow limes, green chillies,
and slices of ginger soaked in brine.

"I made it last week with the limes Kumuda gave me,"
Grandma says.

Kumuda is our neighbour in whose front garden the
lime tree grows. She's a cantankerous woman who has no
patience with children. She's always rude to us and wears a
permanent frown on her face. It comes from not having her
own children, the servants say. I don't remember a time
when our neighbour didn't complain of the noise we made
whenever we played in our compound. We refer to her as
Komodo Dragon—a name coined by Mithuna—rather than
as Kumuda-aunty as well-brought-up children ought to.

"Kumuda's lime tree has started giving fruit all of sudden, it seems," says Aunty. "It looked so hopeless last year."

"From what I heard she followed the advice of some
tantrik, and within months the tree started flowering,"
Grandma says.

"Tantrik!" I exclaim. "Does anyone seek a black-magic
guy's advice in this age?!"

"I wish the tantrik had given her advice on how to have children," Aunty says. "The servants used to joke that her lime tree was as barren as Kumuda."

"If I were you, I wouldn't gossip with servants," Grandma says. Mithuna and I look at each other, and smile.

> Standing foursquare to the elements:
> Shrinking from summer's hot embrace
> Rejoicing in monsoon's wet kisses
> Shrugging off winter's cold shoulder

The afternoon is warm and sultry. The breeze from the distant sea has not yet begun to infiltrate through the cocoanut groves along the shore. Under the creaking fans, we stretch ourselves on straw mats. Aunty also uses a small hand-fan made from fronds of cocoanut palms.

At four o'clock in the evening, I'm awakened by the bustle in the kitchen. Grandma's making evening tea. Aunty gets up reluctantly; she needs to make a show of helping Grandma.

"Where's Mithuna?" she asks, seeing the unoccupied straw mat. "Mithuna! Mithuna!"

I sigh as I also get up and say, "She must have gone up the hill, I'm sure."

"That girl! What's wrong with her!" Grandma says, coming into the room.

"Only you can guess," Aunty says to me, "what your twin sister's up to."

I go outside and make my way to the back of the compound. Scaling the low wall, I scrabble up the hillside. I spot Mithuna. She's scouring the hillside with her palm over her brow to shield her eyes from the afternoon sun.

"Mithuna! Do you still hope to find Whimsy after all these months? Be reasonable," I say.

"There's nothing wrong in hoping," Mithuna says.

On the last day of our holiday last year, Mithuna's pet dog—a small furry Lhasa Apso—went missing. We spent the entire day swarming up and down the hill, shouting for Whimsy until our throats were hoarse. A weeping Mithuna had to be forcibly bundled into the taxi which was taking us to the railway station.

"How can you expect a small pet dog to survive for a year in the wild? Come, let's go back. Grandma is making tea and tiffin for us."

A tired and sweaty Mithuna follows me half-heartedly as I walk away.

"When Daddy said he'd get you another puppy, you should have taken up the offer," I say.

"Like buying a new pen because you misplaced the old one?"

"Sorry, girl. I know, it's not quite as simple as that."

I, too, had liked Whimsy. He was our parents' gift for Mithuna on our thirteenth birthday. I had received an adult-size bicycle. I remember the first day the pup came home. You'd have taken him for a small ball of wool but for the eyes which sparkled when they caught the sunlight from the windows.

When we return to the house, Aunty says with a trace of scorn in her voice: "Did you find your Whisky on the hill?"

"Do I look like a drunkard to you, Aunty?" Mithuna says, in her rare attempt at conversation with elders.

"The name's Whimsy," I say peaceably, "just for the re- cord." At the time when Mithuna christened her pet dog, she was madly into Dorothy Sayers. She's still crazy about mystery novels.

Ignoring us, Aunty fans herself, waiting for the tea and bajjies that Grandma's making.

> In the entire universe,
> Like you there's none
> A creation of some fabulist's pen:
> An ugly duckling of a shrub
> In a twinkling, turns into
> a swan of a tree
> What elixir, what penance or blood sacrifice
> Has wrought this magical makeover?

The next morning after a breakfast of dosas and chutney we lounge in the verandah, sipping coffee from steel tumblers. The sky's downcast, as if on the verge of tears. A cool breeze blows down from the hills, ruffling the treetops.

There's no TV or computer in the house to keep us occupied. For want of anything better to do, Mithuna and I set out to explore the overgrown lot around the house, hoping to spot a snake or stumble upon an anthill.

"Don't go too close to the old well!" Aunty shouts after us, diligent as ever, referring to the disused well with its windlass falling to pieces in the backyard.

We find a pyramid of logs stacked against a back wall. Stuck into a log is an axe. Plucking it out, I start chopping wood just for the heck of it.

After a few minutes, Mithuna says, "May I try, please?"

Glad that Mithuna's at last showing interest in something, I hand her the axe. "Be careful," I say.

Soon we tire of the sport and go back into the house. Mithuna finds herself a detective novel in our late grandfather's old collection, reeking of must and bygone years. Not finding any writers of my choice, I settle for PG Wodehouse, Daddy's favourite author.

> *Dear tree, once you too had been*
> *unwanted, unloved, and barren*
> *But now—*
> *The pride of your mistress's life,*
> *Her triumph, her treasure.*
> *So bountiful, so fecund,*
> *Inviting the evil eye of passersby*

We spend the evening pottering about in the unkempt front garden. Aunty's examining the wild shrubs as if she's a botanist. Nirmala's plucking flowers for the evening pooja.

"How lovely Kumuda's lime tree looks!" Aunty says, gazing up at the tree.

"Doesn't it? Kumudamma is so proud of it," Nirmala says.

"What fascinates me is that it had looked so … so undernourished last year. But look at it now—it's laden with so many fruits!"

"The tantrik's cure did the trick, I suppose."

"What did he recommend?" Aunty asks, all ears.

"You won't believe this. He told her to bury a dead animal under the tree."

"What! But where in the world did Kumuda find a dead animal?" Aunty asks.

"Well, Kumudamma asked Venkatesh, her servant-boy, to help her. As he couldn't find one readily, he killed a small dog he found roaming on the hillside, I believe."

I curse inwardly, as I hear Aunty say, "Dear me, what kind of a dog was it?"

"A small fluffy dog, I was told."

Nirmala goes into the house with her flower-basket overflowing with jasmines, completely oblivious to the stink she has left behind. Mithuna starts wailing, "My dog! My poor dog! That horrible woman had my Whimsy murdered!"

Mithuna begins to run, heading for Komodo Dragon's house. I hurry after her and physically restrain her.

"Lemme go! Lemme go!" Mithuna's screaming all the while. I have a hard time trying to control her.

"Mithuna, why are you shouting?" Grandma asks, suddenly appearing in the verandah as though the commotion has flushed her out of the house.

"Nirmala said that Komodo Dragon got my Whimsy killed!"

"What nonsense!"

"A tantrik told her to bury a dead animal under the lime tree. I want to know if it was my Whimsy."

"But it's late in the evening now," Grandma says. Komodo Dragon's front door is shut, battened down for the night. "I'll talk to her in the morning if you like."

"Your grandmother's right," Aunty says. "Let's not do anything rash."

"Let Grandma handle it," I tell Mithuna. "We are just visitors here. Grandma has to live with her neighbours every day."

Dinnertime is sombre and silent, and Grandmother wisely doesn't serve Komodo Dragon's lime pickle despite Aunty eyeing the jar which stands in a niche. Mithuna eats poorly as usual, but nobody has the heart—or the energy—to nag her. She's quiet, but it's not the quietude that comes from resignation. It's as if she's waiting, treading water until the epic confrontation with Komodo Dragon.

When Mithuna has left the room, Aunty says as she's clearing the dinner things, "It was such a barbaric act. How could Kumuda do it?"

"Being a city-dweller," Grandma says with a pinch of contempt in her voice, "you may not be familiar with the ways of people in small towns. Burying a carcass under a tree is not so uncommon. It's supposed to act as a natural fertilizer. That it was our pet dog is another matter."

The night is restive, like the proverbial lull before storm, and we go to bed early. But around midnight I wake up with a start, not knowing what had roused me. Moonlight filters in obliquely, showing up some furniture, hiding others. Then I hear them—the spasmodic thwacks of a woodcutter. Who would want to chop kindling for the bathroom urn so late in the night?

Then I realize that the sounds are not coming from the back of the house. I rush to the front door—it's unlocked, rattling against the jamb in the wind. When I go out, I see Mithuna's silhouette in the eerie moonlight. She's determinedly hacking at our neighbour's lime tree.

> *A miscreant intent on violence*
> *has unleashed such havoc,*
> *that in one fell swoop*
> *has reduced a legend to dust*

Before I could call out to Mithuna, the scene is ablaze with light. The verandah lamp of Komodo Dragon's house has burst into life. The front door opens, and Komodo Dragon dashes out shrieking, "What are you doing?! What are you doing?!"

"Doing the same thing you did to my Whimsy! What harm had that sweet little dog done to you?!"

"What are you talking about? I know nothing about your dog. You've killed my tree, you wicked girl. I had nursed it back to health as if it were my child. Now I have nothing ... nothing."

"The dog you buried under the tree was like a child to me," Mithuna says.

"I had nothing to do with it! I had entrusted Venkatesh to do the job. I don't even know what he put under the tree!" Komodo Dragon bursts into tears. The ground's littered with fruit, and the tree's bent down, as if bowing its head in shame.

"Why did you have to do such a thing?" I say, leading Mithuna back to the house. "Grandma would have spoken to her."

"Would that have brought my Whimsy back? Would they have thrown Komodo Dragon into prison?"

"If I were you, I'd have let grown-ups handle it."

"You're not me, my dearest twin. I've realized long ago that you can't rely on others to fight your battles. You'll have to do it yourself."

> Grieve not, lime tree
> The scythe of the Reaper
> Awaits us all
> Death's not the end,
> Just a momentary hiatus:
> The seed from your fruit will flower yet again.

The next morning, I wake up with a feeling of dread. But by that time the adults have hijacked our world.

"Get ready quickly," Aunty says. "The taxi will be coming at nine o'clock. We'll have an early breakfast and leave."

"Where are we going?" I ask.

"We are returning to Hyderabad. I spoke to your father. He wanted us to come back immediately."

We have a hastily cooked breakfast made with semolina. When I hear the peremptory *pom-pom!*, I take the suitcases down to the taxi, and load them into the shabby trunk smelling of petrol and God knows what. Grandma comes up to the car. She looks haggard as if she has aged a good many years since last night.

"Do well at school," Grandma says to us. "Forget about what happened yesterday. You have your entire lives ahead of you."

The taxi makes a three-point turn and rumbles down the road, bouncing over the ruts. Waving for the last time, I look back at Grandma. And in our neighbour's garden, there's a barren spot where the lime tree had once so proudly stood, a glowing totem for its mistress.

* * *

That happened a few years ago. People say that going back home is the best part of a journey. But it's not always so, believe me. We were nervous, not knowing what our parents' reaction would be. When we got home, Daddy, assuming a stern voice, told us never to take the law into our own hands. Mummy interjected with the comment that an eye for an eye was not a solution to the world's problems. In the end, for all the stress Mithuna had been through, Daddy bought her another pup, a golden retriever. Mithuna named him Whisky.

Carrion Birds

The spring-gated elevator, hardly bigger than a coffin, took a jet-lagged Naren and his travel-worn luggage to the fifth floor of the apartment block. When he stepped out of the cage, Naren was at a loss on which way to head. There were no markers on the wall. He headed in one direction and then changed tack because the apartment numbers, written in stylized brass, were not leading to P5. Most of the doors of the apartments he passed were closed, but when he approached P5 he heard sounds of plaintive music wafting out and found the door wide open.

He stepped in. Mrinalini, his grandaunt, was lying under the glass lid of a refrigerated metal coffin. She had died of a silent heart attack in her sleep at the age of eighty-two. She had passed the way she had lived: with serene dignity.

The fragrance and smoke of incense sticks were palpably present in the room, like friendly family ghosts. But for the strains of soft devotional music there was silence—even though there were quite a few people milling about. Maybe the people thought if they spoke too loudly or trod too heavily, they may wake the dead. And that wouldn't do at all.

Minni-aunty, lying inert in her coffin, seemed to be bandaged in layers of jasmines and marigolds. She looked frail and shrunken. To Naren, she seemed to wear an expression of mild censure. Naren felt a pang of guilt. He had not cared to visit his grandaunt for so many years, a decade at least.

A woman came up and stood next to him. "She looks so peaceful, doesn't she?" she said. Surprised (do people always see what they wish to see?), Naren turned to look at the person. She was a middle-aged woman wearing a crumpled cotton sari. She looked familiar but he couldn't place her.

"I'm Kamu," she said.

Kamakshi! Now he remembered. She was his first cousin. His father's younger sister's eldest daughter. Advancing years and menopausal weight gain had transfigured her.

"Of course, I know you!"

"You looked as if you didn't recognize me ..."

"No, its not that. I was deep in thought. I was wondering how much Minni-aunty had changed since I last saw her!"

Kamu nodded to the large hand-painted portrait of Minni-aunty hanging prominently on a wall. On a make-shift ledge under the picture, two oil-wick brass lamps glowed. In the old-fashioned portrait, which endeavoured to bring out a photographic realism, Minni-aunty looked vivacious and ebullient. Even in the painting executed by a famous local artist decades ago, there was a sardonic glint to her beaming smile.

"How radiant she looks! I would always tell Minni-aunty that her smile was more brilliant than the jewellery she's seen wearing!"

There was some truth in the statement. The rubies in the picture had a muted gleam, and the necklace itself was of a delicate design, unlike traditional jewellery which tended to be bulky and overwrought. It was something which pleased even the eye of a man who had spent most of his life in the West.

Bharati, his sixty-year-old cousin, spotted him. She was dressed in a neat, pressed sari which was discreetly attractive. She was careful to wear jewellery which was not showy. She had an air of queenly yet sombre elegance. With Minni-aunty's death, she would be appropriating the function of *mater familias* because of her age and position.

She approached Naren with a small smile as big as convention would permit. She gave him a hug, and immediately afterwards dissolved into tears. She was adept at weeping at short notice—she must have had a lot of practice in the last seventy-two hours. He stood in silence, a trifle embarrassed, not knowing what exactly to say or do. He recovered enough poise to rub her back with his left hand—he was still clinging on to his overnight case in his right hand.

After the mandatory tears, she said in a loud whisper, "Narendar, was the plane on time? Did the driver find you easily?"

"Yes, to both questions," Naren said, hoping he could emulate the feat of whispering loudly.

"It was so nice of you to come all the way," Kamu said.

"After all, he was Minni-aunty's favourite nephew," Bharati said.

"Well, she was my favourite aunt, too," Naren said. He had lost both his parents in a car accident when he was fourteen. Though orphaned he had never felt bereft because

Minni-aunty was always there, providing boundless affection and unwavering support.

Naren had taken the first flight out of Vancouver when he heard the news of Minni-aunty's death, arriving in Hyderabad via Hong Kong some twenty hours later. He worked as a General Manager in a plant that made a well-known brand of soap. He had lived more than twenty-five of his fifty years in Canada. He was married to a white woman who worked as a staging professional (someone who redecorated your house when you put it up for sale so that it could fetch a better price than it deserved). They had two daughters who were in university.

Minni-aunty did not have children of her own. And her husband, an unobtrusive and self-effacing man within the house, but a most successful and prominent banker without, had died fifteen years ago—choking over an unexpected bone in a piece of kebab. Both husband and wife had been great benefactors to their relatives, friends and society at large. For instance, they had paid the airfare when Naren went to North America to get a master's degree in science. An act of generosity he could never repay, nor forget.

Bharati introduced him to the people in the room. Some he remembered and some he didn't, though he ought to have because they were purported to be his close relatives. The fact that he had been too long in the West didn't help matters. He felt a little bewildered, as he realized that his extended family had become more extensive with marriages and births since his last visit.

"This is Venkat," Bharati said, introducing him to a balding man in his late fifties. "He's Radha's husband."

"Of course, I remember him! How do you do?" Naren said. People seemed to remember Naren. Was it something to do with his physical appearance? He had the same build he had when he was in his twenties. He had neither gained a lot of weight nor lost a lot of hair. Only his skin had lost its suppleness and his head had acquired a few streaks of grey. Or was it that people in India kept their relatives in mind even if they were out of sight?

"Their son works in New York as a software engineer," said Bharati.

"New*ark*," Venkat, Radha's husband, said.

"Where's Radha?" Naren asked. "It's a long time since I've seen her."

He remembered Radha, a handsome woman in a buxom kind of way, and her son—if he could recall correctly—who whined about everything.

There was an awkward silence for a few moments. Bharati said, "Don't you know? She passed away five years ago ... of a stroke."

"Cardiac arrest," Venkat said.

"I'm sorry," Naren said, though it wasn't clear whether he was apologizing for his gaffe or the passing of Radha.

Pausing only to listen to Naren's often phoney remarks, Bharati went on like an irrepressible tour guide, but pointing out people instead of places: "This is Suresh, he's Parvatamma's son-in-law ... This is Arati, she's Madhukar's wife—they have a six-month-old baby girl ... This is Janakamma, she is Sumati's mother-in-law ..."

Naren's head began to buzz. The aggravation he felt was more than just jetlag.

"I'll take you to your room," Bharati said, when the frenetic throes of introductions finally petered down, not so much because she ran out of people but more because she ran out of breath. As she led him to the room, she said, "You'll be sharing the room with Anand—you know Anand, don't you?"

"Yes, yes," Naren said, despite not knowing Anand from Adam, forestalling any more revelations of the hidden branches of the family tree.

"Luckily, this is a big flat. It has four spacious bedrooms. You wouldn't want to stay in a hotel, would you?"

Truth to tell he might have preferred the alternative, but the family would have considered it an insult of the grossest kind had he checked into a hotel. The apartment block, a stubby tower of concrete, was constructed on the land where Minni-aunty and Ram-uncle's rambling house had stood. The old house had two storeys with large balconies and an expansive roof called a terrace. It didn't have a cohesive structure or façade, as extensions were added on indiscriminately. The house had stood in a half-acre compound and was surrounded by mango and neem trees.

Naren deposited his luggage in a corner of the bedroom. The room was clean and neat. Whoever Anand was, he wasn't an untidy person. A little later, Naren transferred most of the contents of his suitcase to the built-in cupboard. Then he had a bath, standing under a shower of cold water as he was too impatient to wait for the hot water geyser to heat up. He got into a clean set of clothes and stepped out of his bedroom. Immediately upon his entrance, as if waiting for the cue, a maid ambushed him, offering a stainless-steel tumbler full of foaming, piping-hot south-Indian coffee.

The beverage was unbelievably tasty with rich aroma and deep chicory flavour. The very first sip was so resuscitating that he began to feel the languor caused by the long and tiring journey slowly slip away. But he had barely taken a few gulps when it was announced that the minivan that was to convey Minni-aunty to the crematorium had arrived.

Random people sprang up like myrmidons, as if an unseen commander had sounded an inaudible call to rally them. They quickly moved the body on to a makeshift bier, and then carried it down five flights of stairs to the waiting vehicle—an ancient Matador looking barely serviceable and in need of a coat of paint. The dead, Minni-aunty included, weren't expected to be too fastidious.

The women present at the scene began to keen, many surprisingly genuinely, when Minni-aunty was about to start on a journey which was very different from the intercontinental jaunts she had enjoyed in her husband's company. Minni-aunty's body was manoeuvred into the van somehow, after shuffling around the impedimenta which was contained in the van when it was used for purposes other than carting the dead.

Naren got into one of the many cars and SUVs which were brought one after another by chauffeurs to the front of the building. Naren found himself in the company of a middle-aged man and a bunch of young adults—one of Minni-aunty's great-grandnephews named Siddharth and his two friends. The teenagers spoke mostly amongst themselves, discussing disputatiously the selection of the Indian team for the upcoming cricket test matches against Australia.

The middle-aged man introduced himself. "I'm Ganesh, your cousin Sumati's husband." Fortunately for Naren,

Sumati, unlike Radha, was alive and kicking. He remembered that Sumati was an accomplished dancer trained in the traditional style of Bharata Natyam. According to Ganesh, they had two children. The daughter was studying to be a doctor and the son an engineer. Neither of them showed any inclination for either music or dance, but they revelled in listening to English pop music and Bollywood numbers. Ganesh was a chartered accountant working for a multinational company.

"Why don't you perform the last rites for Minni-aunty?" Ganesh asked, out of the blue.

"Me? No!"

"She was so proud of you. She called you a self-made man."

"I don't think I've done anything great in life, other than leaving the country and earning a salary in dollars, and only Canadian at that. Besides, shouldn't someone who was around to take care of Minni-aunty do the honours?"

After driving for three quarters of an hour in the seemingly unruly but harmless traffic of Hyderabad's roads, the cortege turned into a driveway which led to a clutch of low and modernistic buildings. The structures looked as if the builder had abandoned the project halfway through but were attractive in their own minimalist way. This was the crematorium, the launch pad to the next world.

The grounds were full of trees, though not very old. Naren was to learn later that the gardens were laid out conforming to recommendations found in ancient scriptures. Though very much within the city boundaries, it was surrounded by low rock-studded hills dotted with private bungalows.

"Is this something new? The crematorium I went to last time was in Bansilalpet—an old and crowded locality from what I remember. This place looks so neat and clean!" Naren said.

"New brooms sweep well," Ganesh said dismissively. "We had also not heard of it. It was one of the drivers who suggested this crematorium."

"Minni-aunty was always well served by her servants," Naren said.

"That's true. And she, in turn, took good care of them. What goes around comes around. It is the law of Karma."

* * *

Not withstanding his protests, Naren was coerced into performing the last rites. It was determined that Naren was the oldest male relative present descended from Ram-uncle's side of the family.

"Don't worry. We won't make you shave your head and goatee," his nephew Ranjit said with a laugh. Naren was relieved. Those who were bereaved were, by tradition, required to shave off their facial and cranial hair.

He was quickly made to take a shower, once again in cold water, and put on traditional Indian garments—angav-astram and dhoti, two lengths of flowing untailored cloth, one to cover the upper half of the body, the other the nether half. He had to barter away his Levis and Armani golf shirt for good. Still wet from his bath, he did as the priest bade him with words and mime. The rituals reminded Naren of the time when he had performed them for his parents. He had been too bewildered to realize then that he had become an orphan, barely fourteen and all alone in the world. In his hour of need, Minni-aunty and Ram-uncle had stepped in. Today, once again, he felt an orphan. He blinked away the surprising tears that sprang in his eyes.

Holding a burning stave in one hand and an earthen pot of water on his shoulder, Naren made multiple rounds of the body lying on a bed of kindling. When ordered by the priest, Naren, without giving a backward glance, tossed away the pot which broke into shards scattering its contents. Likewise, facing away from the pyre, he reached backwards and lit it. The flames spread slowly and then engulfed the body. A commanding presence when alive, Minni-aunty's lifeless body, like everything else in the universe, would soon be reduced to dust—the very stuff the cosmos was made of. Death, in a way, was a homecoming. Life was but a brief side trip.

Leaving the burning body in the care of the officials of the cremation grounds, they went back to the waiting cars.

There was nothing much to do for the rest of the day, so Naren hung about the house, talking and chatting with relatives, near and distant. Many of the younger ones plied him with queries on immigration. The United States of America, the lodestar for immigrants, was slowly losing its lustre, so the younger generation in whom seeds of migration were sown by society, were turning to other pastures. They sounded chilly towards Canada, seeming to prefer the warmer climates of Australia or New Zealand.

The next morning, it was time to collect the bones and the ashes—having cooled down—so that they could be consigned to a holy river. Naren with Ganesh and a couple of young men, which included Siddharth, who was so critical of the selectors of the Indian cricket team, drove back to the crematorium.

This time the youngsters were analyzing the box office success, or non-success, of the latest film of Shah Rukh Khan the Bollywood star.

"Siddhu sounds like a bright boy," Naren said.

"Yes, he does very well in academics as well as sports. He's doing computer engineering and he's the captain of his college cricket team."

"Uncle, please ..." Siddhu said.

"I suppose, like all bright young men, he will be heading to the US?" Naren said.

"Siddhu wants to stay back and work in India. He thinks there's so much to do here," Ganesh said.

"Uncle, please!"

"I find the younger generation so focussed and idealistic. There's still hope for this country!" Ganesh continued saying.

After reaching the crematorium, there was another round of ceremonies for Naren to sit through. The priest prepared balls of cooked rice as offering to carrion birds. It was of supreme importance that the scavenger birds turned up to partake in the meal. If they did not, it signified that the soul of the person who died was still enmeshed in their mortal coils.

After the ceremonies were done, food on a traditional disposable plate—made with sewn-up dried leaves—was taken to a vantage point and offered to birds. Mostly crows, though on occasion, competing hawks and eagles, were expected to feast on them.

The sky was bright and clear; while one could hear the bird calls of smaller avian species, none of the big players seemed to be around.

"They will come," the priest said. "It may take some time though."

They cooled their heels in the nearby visitor's room, but no birds came. Naren began to feel hot and thirsty. He had left his mineral water bottle in the car. He felt a bit stressed, too—he knew he was expected to travel to a holy river, miles and miles away, to scatter the ashes.

Ganesh had said, like a maître d' suggesting a choice of dishes, "You could travel north of Hyderabad where the Godavari flows. Or you could travel south to the Krishna. You could also disperse the ashes at Mantralayam on the Tungabhadra."

"Which of these trips can be done in the shortest possible time?" Naren asked. After he asked the question, he hoped he didn't sound too brusque. Living in North America can blunt one's sensibilities.

Ganesh's eyebrows rose a little, but he said, "River Krishna at Beechupally ... But it would be nice if you could scatter the ashes at Mantralayam. Though it is the farthest of the three, Minni-aunty always liked to visit Raghavendra Swamy's shrine in Mantralayam."

"Whatever you say," Naren said. "Mantralayam, here I come."

The entire trip would take ten to twelve hours on roads which were unpredictable—sometimes comparable to those in North America, sometimes unimaginably bad. But travel he must, however arduous. This was going to be his posthumous gift to Minni-aunty.

The manager of the crematorium handed over a terra-cotta urn containing the ashes and unburnt portions of Minni-aunty's bones. Much to Naren's relief, Ganesh decided to return to the apartment, without waiting to see first-hand if the crows had a bite of the offering. But he enjoined more than requested Siddhu to stay back and wait for the crows. The young man seemed a bit put off but didn't seem to mind too much as a car was left at his disposal and he had his friends for company.

They returned to the apartment, hot and hungry. The pot with the remains was left outside in the hallway. It was considered inauspicious to take funerary ashes into the house proper. It was decided that the ashes would be dispersed on the following day, after consulting the almanac for an auspicious hour.

In the living room, people had scattered themselves on all available pieces of furniture. There was an attractive sofa set made of solid old teak which had been newly upholstered. Being a carry-over from a statelier past, it looked a bit too large for the living room of the apartment. There were a few basket chairs made with plastic rattan and a collection of cushioned stools made of intricately carved wood.

The gathering had decided to wait for news of the crows' arrival before they themselves had lunch. It was considered blasphemous to start tucking into Minni-aunty's favourite foods before the carrion birds had their fill.

They were disappointed that Ganesh didn't have any news and they had to wait for confirmation from Siddhu. With mounting hunger, they sat around idly chatting, hoping that tidings of crows descending on the offering would come soon. The afternoon was becoming warmer and the ceiling fan was spinning on the highest possible setting. The desultory conversation eventually led to the topic which was on the minds of everyone present: Minni-aunty's last will and testament.

Nobody, apart from the family lawyer, knew of its contents better than Bharati. She was not only privy to Minni-aunty's plans and intentions, but she was also named the executor of the will. It was Ganesh who goaded her: "There's so much suspense being built up, and there are so many rumours flying about. Would you be able to clear them by shedding some light on it?"

"The lawyer is going to call a formal meeting with all the major legatees. It wouldn't be correct on my part to pre-empt him," Bharati said.

"You need not go into all the details, you know. Just a small preview will do," Venkat said.

"Like a movie trailer," Ganesh said drily. Turning to Naren, he whispered, "The way all the relatives have been living off your Minnie-aunty, it's a wonder there's anything left to distribute!"

"I will only divulge this," Bharati said, "the bulk of her estate has been given away to charities, especially ones dealing with children's issues, like orphanages, organizations taking care of street children, and children of bonded labourers."

A collective hush descended on the room, signalling that all who had gathered there were more than a bit disappointed.

"By doing so, she has made all of us orphans," someone murmured.

"Bharati, you used the word 'bulk,'" Ganesh said, who was prone to splitting hairs, "I suppose it means that not the entire fortune has been given away? Could there be smaller bequests to family members?"

"I am unable to recall all the details—it is a pretty exhaustive list. This much I can say: she has bequeathed her jewellery, her expensive saris, costly knick-knacks, and pieces of art to her relatives, friends and servants."

"But no gifts of money to them?" Arati asked, a petite and pretty grandniece who worked as a subeditor at a local paper—everyone knew writing was no longer a paying enterprise.

"She has definitely apportioned small amounts to all the relatives she has known personally. She has set aside a not-insubstantial amount of cash and jewellery for the executor to give out in case Minni-aunty has overlooked someone inadvertently or if anybody has a pressing need. One thing I can say for sure, nobody in this room has been forgotten."

"How much money can we expect?" Suresh asked, a software engineer working at the development centre of either Microsoft or Apple—Naren couldn't remember which. It was rumoured that he drew a princely sum as salary.

"I don't think I should go into that. But don't get your hopes too high!" Bharati said.

"Come on, give us a ballpark figure. At least a range if you don't want to divulge what is in the will," Suresh said.

"Anything between one lakh and five lakhs of rupees," Bharati answered.

"One lakh is only about two thousand Canadian dollars," Ganesh whispered into Naren's ear.

"One lakh! What can you get for one lakh? Not even a fricking moped let alone a motorcycle!" Ranjit said, who worked as a medical rep and visited doctors on his two-wheeler trying to sell patent medicine his American employer made.

"Who knows? You could get five lakhs, Ranjit. Don't be such a pessimist!" Kamu said.

"Guys, I just want to caution you all," Bharati said. "The sum of money Minni-aunty has set aside for each one of you is inversely proportional to your social status and family wealth. This means the more fortunate one is, the less he or she will get. All the people who will be receiving close to five lakhs are mostly servants and the less fortunate among our friends and relatives."

"How would Minni-aunty know about the net worth of each one of us?" Ranjit asked. All eyes turned towards Ganesh.

"I had nothing to do with it! Minni-aunty didn't consult me when she made the will!" Ganesh said.

"Being her closest relative, I was looking forward to inherit quite a big chunk of her property," Anand said, disgust running deep in his voice. "At my age, a windfall would have been most welcome." Anand, who lived in a small town a couple of hundred miles from Hyderabad, was generally believed to be the owner of a sizeable chunk of real estate—three residential and two commercial properties. He was forever seeking ways and means to enlarge his holdings. He added: "This trip to Hyderabad has been a waste of time and money."

"It's not about money, you know," Naren said, trying to mitigate the general disappointment. "Her bequest, big or small, is a symbol of her affection. The important thing to keep in mind is that she has she remembered you in her will."

"It's easy for you to say that. You lead a cushy life in Canada! You have Medicare, government pension and unemployment insurance," Ranjit said. "We have to rot here in this country."

"But he also has to face Canada's winters," Ganesh said.

"I would happily trade Indian summers, where one gets roasted at temperatures above forty-five degrees centigrade, for Canadian winters any day for the kind of living standards they have!"

"What about the jewellery?" Latha, Ranjit's wife, asked. She had two daughters, so she was forever squirreling away money for the daughters' dowry and wedding expenses.

"Minni-aunty, as you know, didn't crave for fineries of life. She didn't buy much jewellery for herself. But what she inherited from her parents and her in-laws she has given away using her well-known principle of equity: those who have less will get more. Having all said and done, it will not amount to much."

"Who's getting the diamond set?" Sumati asked.

A pall of silence descended, like the lull in the background score of a scary movie before the director throws a terrifying scene at the unwary audience. Bharati cleared her throat. But before she could speak, Ganesh said, "It's a sort-of tip given by Minni-aunty for being the executor of the will."

"So, you are one of the unfortunate relatives, eh?" Madhukar, Arati's husband, said. He was a doctor working in a small private hospital.

"Fuck the jewellery!" Ranjit said. "Who gets the cars?"

At that very moment Siddhu entered the room. Though he must have been carrying the much-awaited news of the feathered predators, the assemblage was more engrossed in

Bharati's revelations to take notice. Siddhu looked sweaty and wore an expression which was both bored and sullen.

Bharti recovered her poise and said, "She has left them to the drivers."

Wondering why the crowd didn't hail his arrival as he had expected, Siddhu stood listening to the ongoing conversation, as if he hadn't outgrown the dictum drilled into him by his parents: children are meant to be seen not heard.

"Even the Merc!" Ranjit said.

"Her reasoning is that once she passes away, they will not have a good job. The drivers could run their cars as taxi service or Uber or whatever."

"That Rajaiah! He will sell the Honda City and drink away all the money," Sumati said

"What he does with his legacy is not our business," Ganesh said

"Hasn't Minni-aunty made any special bequests?" Arati said, as if she was hoping against hope.

"Yes. She has left her portrait which is hanging in this room to Kamakshi," Bharati said, "in lieu of any gifts of cash."

For once Kamu was at a loss for words. She looked shell-shocked.

"I'm not surprised," Ranjit said with a chuckle. "The way Kamu-aunty would go on about how regal Minni-aunty looked in the portrait!"

"The portrait is quite valuable. It was done by a famous painter. I can't recall his name. Surya something," Bharati said.

Kamu's expression seemed to quicken, and the zombie-look began to fade.

"How much would it sell for?" Ganesh asked.

"I wouldn't know for sure. Around five lakhs or so, I guess," Bharati said. Kamu's face brightened visibly.

"But nothing compared to the ruby necklace Kamu-aunty was angling for!" Ranjit said.

"That's not true!" Kamu said. "I … I feel privileged and honoured that Minni-aunty chose to bestow the gift of the portrait on me."

At that point, Naren, who until then was a mostly mute onlooker, was suddenly seized by an inexplicable urge. Later he couldn't understand how he allowed such a base instinct to get the better of him. He said, "Bharati, while we are all on the subject … if it's possible, I'd like to take a small memento back with me … something to remind me of Minni-aunty."

"Why of course!" Bharati said. "Do you have anything particular in mind, Naren?"

Naren said haltingly, "You know the necklace Minni-aunty is seen wearing in the portrait? Though of a simple design, it's still so attractive. It looks like just the thing Jennifer might like …"

"The Burmese rubies!" Kamu exclaimed.

Bharati looked as if she was doing sums in her head. Ranjit rolled his eyes. Sumati snorted. Venkat peered at Naren. Anand raised his arms heavenwards.

Ganesh, who had formed a kinship with Naren, piped up. "I hope Bharati will agree. It is the least we can do for a person who came all the way from Canada to perform the last rites, even though he was not a blood relative of Minni-aunty."

"Big deal," Naren heard someone murmur.

"I can't give an answer right away, Naren. I might have to consult the lawyer."

Suresh, with pangs of hunger gnawing into him, said, "Screw the rubies! Siddhu's here. Bro, what news do you bring? I'm hungry as a hunter!"

"Did you see any crows feed on the offering?" Bharati asked, relieved to be diverted.

"No ... I waited for more than two hours. In fact, I didn't see even one bird hovering in the sky," Siddhu said.

Kamu gasped. "That's not a good sign!"

"Are we supposed to starve to death?" Ranjit said.

"You mean not even a single bird came to eat?" Bharati said. "Where could all the crows have gone?" She looked with dismay at Siddhu.

Siddhu started to scan the room, pausing for an infinitesimal moment at Naren, before moving on.

"Do you really want to know, Bharati-aunty?" Siddhu said. "I, for one, can make a good guess as to where you can find them."

Storm in a Teacup

The train was already at the platform, its entire length besieged by visitors who had come to see off friends and relatives. Rajesh stole a quick glance at his watch and quickened his pace.

Like any other railway junction in India, Vijayawada pulsated with action and noise. A nasally voice was making announcements in three languages; a string of overhead TV sets was belting out commercials without pause; hawkers were barking at the top of their voices; adding to this din was the constant clangour of the trains themselves—coming, going or merely shunting in the sidings.

Rajesh was a wiry young man in his late twenties. There was something about him that set him apart from the people around him. Perhaps it was the veneer of sophistication that comes from having lived for a long time in a western country, even though he was wearing a pair of faded blue jeans and a cream golf shirt. A small duffel bag was slung from one of his shoulders, and he dragged behind him a suitcase that had airline labels stuck on it. The station was hot and humid, and Rajesh, his armpits damp with sweat, pushed his way through the crowd. Side-stepping pushcarts laden with plastic knick-knacks and stepping over gunny-wrapped parcels strewn on the ground, he reached his air-conditioned coach.

When he got in, the outside heat and noise were cut off with a guillotine-like swiftness. This was a completely different world: the air was sweet and cool, laced with a faint smell of faux leather. Rajesh took a seat by a window and stowed his bags under the berth. The seat opposite him was occupied by a middle-aged man engrossed in a novel. Perhaps becoming aware of Rajesh's scrutiny, the man looked up.

"Hi!" Rajesh said.

The man nodded gravely and returned to his book.

Soon the train gave a lurch and began to move, clucking its tongue as it rolled over the points. Rajesh pulled out a copy of *India Today* from his bag and flipped through it. When he was finished with the magazine, he put it aside, and tried to occupy himself by looking out the window. All he saw through the tinted pane was a formless landscape sluggishly swimming by. When Rajesh turned his face away, resigned to the prospect of a boring and uneventful journey, he noticed his fellow traveller shutting the book.

"Not liking the book?" Rajesh asked.

The man gave the barest hint of a smile. "You're right. The story is so far-fetched. Almost unbelievable. Luckily it's fiction!"

"Makes good holiday reading, I suppose!"

"I am not on holiday," the man said.

"Oh! What brought you to Vijayawada? Business?" Rajesh asked.

"I was there to give a talk at a public meeting," the man said. "What about yourself?"

"I'm on vacation. I am returning to Hyderabad."

"Do you live there?" the man asked, as if not believing.

What is it, thought Rajesh, about me that makes local people suspect that I don't belong here? I am as much an Indian as anyone else.

"Yes. I work there, but I am from Toronto," said Rajesh.

"Oh," the man said, looking away, as if losing interest in the conversation.

Did I sound a bit uppity when I mentioned Toronto? Rajesh wondered. He had discovered that a few Indians, especially of the Leftist persuasion, had a mistrust of the Western world.

Rajesh persisted. "What did you speak on, if I may ask, at the public meeting?"

The man reluctantly drifted back into the conversation, saying primly, "The prevalence of superstition in our society."

"That's awesome! It sounds so fascinating!"

"I'm Dr. Suryam," the man said, as though capitulating, "Professor of Nuclear Physics."

"I'm Rajesh. I work as an international law professional for a Canadian company doing business in India."

"Interesting. I belong to a group of rationalists. We try to educate the public on the perils of superstition," Dr. Suryam said. "The country is full of swamis, gurus, astrologers, palmists, and what have you."

"We Indians certainly are a gullible lot," Rajesh said.

"You're right. Until the entire populace is made to think rationally, we will not be able to get rid of these charlatans," Dr. Suryam said. Once he was astride his hobby horse, there was no stopping him. "Right from the moment a child is born, it is indoctrinated into this nonsense. Even before the mother steps out of the hospital, the family has the horoscope cast for the child! As to marriages, just don't ask. Some people can't get married because they have a bad horoscope."

"That's not good," Rajesh said.

"Then they say perform this ritual or that ritual, all of them expensive, and somehow the horoscope sets itself right! They are all out to cheat innocent people. Bloody humbugs!"

"I hope I don't run into any of them!"

"One never knows. I myself had a very unfortunate experience some years ago ..."

* * *

... After completing a BSc degree from Osmania University, I took up the job of a medical rep. Although my father had wanted me to go abroad for higher studies, he eventually came around and even bought me a motorcycle to help me with my work. A two-wheeler was a must if you wanted to be a salesman of any kind.

The motorcycle also came in handy when I was dating a girl called Tara. She was not much of a looker but she was full of life and had oodles of talent. She was doing her BA in English Literature at Nizam College. To a guy who read only the pharmacopoeia, for profit as well as pleasure, she seemed so fascinating. Tara was into everything, from aerobics to Zen Buddhism. But her chief interest was astrology. She couldn't utter two sentences together without making a reference to one Zodiac sign or the other. Her conversation was peppered with phrases like "How like a Leo!" or "Such a typical Gemini."

So, dating Tara meant mostly picking her up from wherever her current interest took her. Sometimes the stadium, sometimes the auditorium, sometimes the museum, sometimes the planetarium. Afterwards, we would go to a small restaurant or an ice-cream parlour. Later in the evening, I would drop off Tara at her house. Her father would be pacing the verandah in his striped pyjamas, waiting for Tara to return.

After finishing my evening round one day, I rode up to the place where Tara and her friends were rehearsing for a play. Tara was waiting for me outside, surrounded by a cluster of her adoring friends. I could recognize her laughter even before the headlamp of my motorbike caught her in its beam.

"Hi," Tara said. She added, in mock anger: "You're late."

"I'm sorry!" I said. "But once in a while I've got to show up at work, you know."

"Suri, you've already met Usha and Salim," said Tara. "Meet my new friend, Javier. He's from Canada. He's here in Hyderabad on an exchange program. He's a Sagittarian, by the way."

"No, no," Javier protested, "I'm a non-vegetarian."

"Good for you," I said. I turned to Tara and asked, "Has the casting been finalized?" Tara and her friends were planning to stage *Blithe Spirit*.

"Not as yet," Tara said, hopping on to the bike. "Bye, guys!"

As we sped away, she said, "You shouldn't have asked that question. Poor Usha, she might get left out this time. I'll be playing Madame Arcati, in all probability."

"How was I to know that?" I said. "But that's bad. She was excellent in *Arsenic and Old Lace*, wasn't she?"

"Well, the newspapers didn't think so," Tara said sharply. "No doubt some men get carried away by her looks."

We were bouncing along a bad stretch of road, and Tara for some reason clung to me more tightly than was entirely necessary.

"By the way, I've heard of this lady in Begumpet," Tara said. "She does tea leaf reading. She's supposed to be quite a character. I want to meet her."

"Why? To find out if your play will be a success?"

"Don't be stupid. I want to study her mannerisms. It will help me with my role."

"Good God, going around studying people! You must be mad," I said.

"There's a method to my madness!" she said with a laugh. "I'll ring up Mrs. Batliwala and book an appointment for Sunday afternoon."

"Sunday afternoon?" I asked. "I thought we were going to the cinema!"

"I've changed my mind," Tara said. "Tell me, are you taking me to Mrs. Batliwala or not?"

"All right, all right," I said.

On Sunday, when I went to pick up Tara, she appeared with a couple of her fellow troupers in tow. Climbing on to the pillion, she called out, "Bye Boris! Bye Salim!"

As we rode away, Tara said, "I'm so happy for Boris, he's got Bradman's part."

"Now, who's Boris?" I asked.

"Why, he's the guy from Canada," Tara said. "I introduced him to you the other day."

"If I remember right, his name started with an H."

"J, actually. The other guys found his first name too difficult to pronounce, so they shortened his last name, Borrasca, to Boris. He is Spanish, really. Though he lives in Canada, his family hails from South America."

"You seem to know a lot about this chap."

"Are you feeling J?" Tara said, laughing.

We neared the tea leaf reader's house and Tara hollered, "Stanislavksy, here I come!"

"I thought you said her name was Batliwala," I said, turning off the engine.

Tara jumped off the motorbike. She gave me a peck on my cheek and said, "My dearest but practical Capricornian! Forget about Mr. Stanislavsky. Just concentrate on your patent medicines."

Mrs. Batliwala lived in an old, tile-roofed bungalow surrounded by neem and mango trees. The house looked as if it had taken a step back to accommodate an empty moss-covered pond in the front. The property must have seen better times but now it had an aura of neglect. As Tara and I walked up to the front door we heard a dog bark somewhere in the house. I rang the bell.

A peculiar voice shouted, "Fuck off! Fuck off!" Taken aback, Tara and I looked at each other. Beyond the closed door, we heard a woman say, "Stop it, Freni!"

The door was flung open, and a plump, elderly lady appeared at the doorway. She was dressed in a flowing gown, and a quantity of chains encircled her throat. A white Pomeranian pranced around her legs, barking belligerently at us as though we were Bonnie and Clyde.

"You must be Tara," Mrs. Batliwala said, smiling. "Welcome ..." Her words were drowned in a flutter of wings as a parakeet flew in and settled on Mrs. Batliwala's shoulder. The bird rasped, "Get lost, you buggers!"

Mrs. Batliwala said, "Come along, my dears. Let's go into my study. I must apologize for Freni's language. Poor thing. It is not her fault. One of my servants taught Freni the most abominable language."

We followed Mrs. Batliwala as she waddled ahead of us, her shoes clacking like castanets on the marble floor. The house was chockablock with antique furniture, and I was struck by the profusion of handmade lace. There was a patina of dust on the furniture and the lace was turning yellow with age.

"This is my friend, Suri," Tara said as we sat down at a round rosewood table. Mrs. Batliwala smiled and gave me a knowing look. Even as Tara and Mrs. Batliwala indulged in small talk, I couldn't help thinking of the countless visitors who must have sat at the very place, anxious to have their future revealed.

Now and then, Mrs. Batliwala would throw a question at me. But even before I could give an answer, off she would go, talking of something else.

Turning her face to me, she'd ask, "Do you find your work interesting?"

"Well—" I said.

"Come to Mummy, my dear Sir Lancelot," Mrs. Batliwala interjected.

"... I beg your pardon?"

The Pomeranian, in response to his mistress's invitation, jumped onto her lap. Mrs. Batliwala continued her desultory conversation for some time until at last she said,

"I'll make some tea for you all. It's going to be just tea without milk or sugar for you, Tara. Don't expect chai."

As if responding to a stage prompt, Sir Lancelot leaped off his siege perilous and scurried away. Mrs. Batliwala rose and went up to a table at the far end of the room to switch on a kettle.

"I get the leaves specially from Ceylon," Mrs. Batliwala said. "None of your Red Label / Yellow Label stuff for me."

She walked over to us carrying a tray laden with gold-trimmed china. She placed a strainer, a bowl of sugar cubes and a small jar of milk in front of me. "Only for you," she said. She poured out the tea from a teapot and proffered the cup to Tara, saying, "Drink it up, dear. Hold the cup with both your hands. Be silent as you drink. Just remember to leave a teeny-weeny drop at the bottom."

I made myself some weak-looking tea and took a gulp. I almost choked. That's how bad it was. Tara took small sips with an air of a master taster.

Freni swept down into the room and landed on Mrs. Batliwala's shoulder.

Tara finished her tea and placed the cup in the middle of the table. Mrs. Batliwala gently picked up the cup and gazed into its heeltaps.

"Lovely!" Mrs. Batliwala exclaimed. "I see many flowers, a whole garland of them! You are a lucky girl! You have a great future ahead of you. It's roses, roses all the way. I see a long and happy married life for you ..."

Mrs. Batliwala raised her head and cast a meaningful glance at me. She continued, "No trouble there ... I see two bonnie babies. One boy and one girl. You'll also have a successful career ... something to do with commerce or management. You'll go abroad, too. You won't be living in India, that's for sure."

As Mrs. Batliwala stared into the teacup, her face began to darken. "Wait a minute!" she said. "My! Everything looks so blurry. I see something like ... like a storm in here. Dear me!"

Freni gave a loud cackle and flew away. She began to circle overhead like a fighter plane on a recce. Sir Lancelot gave a short loud bark and raced out of the room. Mrs. Batliwala stopped looking into the cup and lifted her head. She tried to muster a smile but failed. She returned to her cup.

After peering into it, she said, "How amazing! It all looks so normal, now! My eyes must have been playing tricks on me. I'm sorry if I alarmed you. In tea leaf reading, first impressions are the best impressions. As I said, you have a great future ahead of you."

She turned to me and said, "You both make such a fine pair! There's nothing to worry about. Really, nothing to worry at all."

Tara rose to her feet and thanked Mrs. Batliwala absently, as if her mind was far away.

When I offered her fifty rupees, Mrs. Batliwala said, "There's no need, believe me." But she allowed herself to be easily persuaded to accept the money.

On our way back, I said, "How was your tea leaf reader?"

"Great," replied Tara, from behind me on the pillion. "How was your tea?"

"Bad to the last drop," I said. "I thought that she had put some arsenic in it."

Tara did not react for a few seconds. And then, suddenly, she burst out laughing. She wrapped her arms around me and said, "I really love you."

In the days that followed, Tara got busy with rehearsals and I had to pick her up every evening, right from the proscenium.

The play itself was a success, and Tara's performance got good notices. She was on cloud nine.

But for me, life was not turning out to be a bed of roses. My long-suffering boss, unhappy with my performance, threatened to sack me. To make matters worse, my motorcycle was stolen, and the insurance company was taking its own sweet time to pay up.

But all this was nothing. One fine day, Tara dumped me. Just like that, without so much as a by-your-leave. She seemed to vanish into thin air. I ran from pillar to post. But without my motorcycle, it was so damn difficult. Her parents were cagey—downright uncooperative, if I may say so. They wouldn't let out anything other than the fact that she was out of the country.

I had never felt so unhappy and depressed in my life before. I was so devastated that I wanted to weep. And I did shed a few tears, which made me feel ashamed, small and angry. "Get a grip on yourself," I told myself. My affair with Tara was over. *Finis*. Never again would I offer to pick up Tara, unless it was to bring her remains from a crematorium. On second thoughts, not even then. I'd rather let that Boris-fellow do the job.

Years later I came to know that Tara had married Boris and left for Canada.

* * *

"... Is it any surprise that I have no patience with these fortune tellers?" Dr. Suryam said, ending his story.

"No," Rajesh replied, sympathy stirring within him for this rather pompous-seeming fellow passenger. "I can understand how you feel."

"I coughed up fifty rupees for her asinine predictions. And looked such a fool in the bargain," Dr. Suryam said, his voice betraying the pain and humiliation he had experienced so many years ago.

"That's life, eh?" Rajesh said. "But it's interesting that Tara lives in Canada."

"When you mentioned Toronto, the word cut me to the quick—even after all these years!"

The train slowed down to a crawl. It was nearing its destination. Rajesh pulled out his duffel bag from under the seat. He said, "I know of a Tara who is from Hyderabad. She's a branch manager at Bank of Montreal. But she's much too young to be the person you mentioned. Anyways, I don't think her last name is ..."

"Borrasca," Dr. Suryam said. "The guy was called Javier Borrasca."

"Borrasca ..." Rajesh said, as if swilling the word around in his mouth. "Do you know what Borrasca means in Spanish?"

Dr. Suryam shook his head. Suddenly, the coach seemed to become full of people: passengers milled around in the passageway while the attendants scuttled about retrieving empty teapots and whatnot. Even though the train was in motion, the red-shirted coolies were already inside, elbowing their way down the corridor. Dr. Suryam and Rajesh rose and pulled out their suitcases from under the seats.

"Borrasca means a storm," Rajesh said. "So that's what the old girl saw in the teacup, I suppose. She wasn't so wide off the mark, after all!"

The train came to a halt. Rajesh edged sideways, trying to find a gap in the unending flow of passengers in the corridor. Turning his head, Rajesh said, "It was nice talking to you. And goodbye."

Dr. Suryam gave no reply. Standing as though rooted to the spot, he looked dazed.

Nachurees Ten Rupees

The road leading out of Hyderabad became progressively narrower and more uneven, and soon it disappeared altogether. The jeep bounced along an unpaved track, slowing every now and then to yield to a herd of goats or buffaloes.

The landscape was still lush with monsoon grass, and the outcrops of rock—typical of the Deccan plateau—stood out like crazily sculpted exhibits of an artist gone berserk. Now and then, a spire of a small Hindu temple or a cupola of a Moslem tomb sprang into view. At one place, a row of power-transmission towers strode across the scene like interloping giants, upsetting the picture of pristine purity.

"We will be there soon. Our house is just beyond the next village," Anil told Rajesh.

Rajesh was a young man who had grown up in Toronto, though he was born in India. His family had migrated to Canada when he was still a child. Now, twenty years later, his job as a consultant had brought him back to India. Anil was his colleague in the company that was installing telecom equipment in many parts of India. When Anil had invited Rajesh to spend Diwali at their family residence outside the city, Rajesh, who remembered very little of his life in India, had enthusiastically accepted the invitation.

The jeep geared down to a crawl as it passed through the village. Garish advertisements for fertilizers, PVC pipes and other similar products were emblazoned on the walls of the buildings that were skirting the road. A couple of pi-dogs ran alongside the jeep barking ferociously and fell back only when they had got tired of the sport.

"And that's our house," said Anil.

Rajesh looked up and saw the large, imposing building, built with brick and lime plaster, presiding over the village. Its coat of whitewash had begun to blacken with age. A crenellated wall, pierced by a tall gateway with large wooden doors, surrounded the house. Passing through the open gateway, the jeep raced up the driveway and screeched to a halt under the portico. The driver sounded the horn like a flourish of trumpets to announce their arrival.

Anil's parents, their faces beaming, came out of the house to welcome them.

"This is my friend, Rajesh," Anil said, introducing him.

Mr. Rao extended his hand to Rajesh, saying, "I'm Anil's dad."

"I hope you had a pleasant ride," Mrs. Rao said.

"It was awesome," Rajesh said. "The countryside is so beautiful."

A servant appeared from nowhere like a genie and commandeered their luggage. Anil's parents led them into the house. The drawing room was big and dark, and had a faint, dank smell. It was full of old and heavy furniture made of rosewood—carry-overs from a bygone age. There was a showcase housing knick-knacks from all over the world. An ornate brass swing hung from the ceiling in one part of the room. Stuffed heads of tigers and deer-like ant-lered animals ranged high up along the wall.

Anil chose to seat himself on the swing, which at once began to sway and emit a metallic mewling. The rest of them sat down on the sofas arranged around a large centre table that had a profile of a lion carved on each of its legs, Mrs. Rao asked, "Would you like to have some coffee?"

Even before he could answer the question, a maid appeared holding a tray bearing steaming cups of coffee. After taking the tray around, she asked Mrs. Rao loudly in Telugu, "Is this young man from Delhi?"

"No," Rajesh said, who understood the language but could speak it only haltingly.

"You can speak Telugu! Then the place you come from wouldn't be as far away as Delhi!" she said. Obviously, New Delhi, India's capital situated in the north was the ultima thule in her mind.

Mrs. Rao laughed. "He is from a place called Toronto. It's very much farther than Delhi, Kamala," Turning to Rajesh, she asked, "Which part of Telangana do your parents come from?"

"Warangal. I have uncles and cousins living there."

"It's not far away from here."

"I'm planning to visit it soon."

"My brother lives in Detroit," Mr. Rao said, "It's very close to the Canadian border, isn't it?"

"Yes, but I have never been there," Rajesh said.

"We visited the US a few years ago. We saw the Niagara Falls from the American side though," Mrs. Rao said.

As they were talking, a man in his late thirties slipped into rather than entered the room. He was sloppily dressed and moved about in a jerky and clumsy manner.

"This is Kanna, my youngest brother," Mr. Rao said.

"How do you do?" Kanna said with a voice which was thick and lispy at once.

Kanna picked up a cup and sat down on a sofa. He drank the coffee in quick, slurpy gulps.

When they finished having coffee, Anil said to Rajesh, "Let me take you to your room."

Anil led Rajesh deep into the house and took a narrow stairway to reach the upper floor. The bedroom was sparingly furnished. A wrought-iron cot festooned with a mosquito net stood under a large ceiling fan. The cotton mattress, covered with white bed linen, looked fluffy and cool. The only window in the room had only the upper shutters open. There were some books standing on the windowsill, leaning on the side wall. The room smelled faintly of grain and gunnysacks.

When Anil left, Rajesh went up to the window and gazed out. The room overlooked a large yard. He could see a vegetable patch surrounded by shrubs bearing small tropical flowers. There were many tall trees, such as poplar and mango, casting their cool shadows in the afternoon sun. At the far end of the compound there was a row of small houses, more like tenements. In the distance, beyond the wall, he could see fields of paddy.

Suddenly there was a flash of colour as a group of children, dressed in clothes of every shade, came half-running across the yard. There were about half-a-dozen of them and they seated themselves in a circle under the shade of a mango tree. Clapping their hands, they began to chant, "Nachurees, ten rupees, will you please, name some ..."

"Animals!" the eldest girl sang out. "Such as lion, be quick!"

"Tiger, be quick!" the girl sitting next to her said.

"Cow, be quick!" a small boy next in the pecking order said.

"Raju, be quick!" another boy said with a snigger.

"That's wrong! You get a D! You get a D!" another boy shouted, who must have had the name Raju.

"Anand, that's very mean of you," the eldest girl said.

"Why? Raju always ends up becoming the donkey."

"Now you get a D. Don't protest or you'll get an O as well," she said. "Pushpa, it's your turn now."

The children began to sing, "Nachurees, ten rupees, will you please, name some ..."

"Flowers!" Pushpa shouted. "Rose, be quick!"

"Jasmine, be quick!"

"Lotus, be quick!"

The children continued to chant and play while Rajesh went back to his bed and lay down. An hour later, he freshened himself and went back down. There was a lot of hustle and bustle about the house, and a pervading smell of joss sticks and smoke from the fireworks. The front of the house seemed to be full of noise and light. As he stepped out, he saw colourful flashes, accompanied by thunderclaps of sound. Anil walked up to him and asked, "Did you manage to get some rest. I heard my cousins playing in the yard. I hope they didn't make too much noise."

"Not this much," Rajesh said, as he looked at the same children running about with lighted sparklers in their hands, laughing and shouting, adding to the din of the firecrackers.

"Nowadays, Diwali is more of a festival of sound than of light," Anil said.

"Anyways, the place looks great! Almost like a fairy land," Rajesh said.

The entire façade of the house was aglow with the shivering light from scores of small clay lamps. They were everywhere: they ran along the parapets, perched on the windowsills, and trickled down the steps.

Rajesh took the lighted sparkler offered by Anil. He held it for some time, before throwing away the spent, burnt-out stick. He watched as Anil and his cousins fired 'rockets' and 'bombs' with joyous abandon.

Around eight o'clock they went in for dinner. The dining room was confoundingly full of people—all uncles, aunts and cousins of Anil who were visiting for Diwali—and Rajesh, feeling like an ass, smiled and nodded as he was introduced to each one of them. The dining table was crowded with stainless steel vessels filled with all kinds of food.

As Rajesh helped himself from the buffet, Anil's mother said, "It's all vegetarian food. I hope you don't mind?"

"Not at all, and I like Indian vegetarian food."

"It is a relief to hear that," she said.

"I heard that Diwali is the start of the traditional New Year," Rajesh said.

"No, not for people in this part of the country," she said. "It's celebrated as New Year's Day only in some parts of western and northern India."

"Even then, as a tradition many Indian businessmen all over the country open their account books during Diwali," Mr. Rao said, joining in. "Lakshmi, the goddess of wealth is worshipped on Diwali."

"Lord Rama returned on the day of Diwali from Lanka and the lamps were lit up in Ayodhya to welcome him. You've heard of the Ramayana, haven't you?" Mrs. Rao asked.

"Of course. I've read a very abridged version of it," Rajesh replied.

"Today, the night before Diwali, is very auspicious, too," Mrs. Rao said. "It's the day when one of Lord Krishna's wives destroyed a demon called Naraka."

"Jeez! The traditions and festivals of India always bewilder me!" Rajesh said.

"Not to worry," Mrs. Rao said. "Though we live in India, often we feel the same."

After dinner, and much leave-taking, Rajesh went up to his room. From the row of books placed on the windowsill, he selected one called *Great Cases of Scotland Yard*. When he finished the chapter on Neil Cream, he switched off the light. In the dark the sounds of the night seemed to grow louder. He could hear the electric thrumming of the cicadas outside. Frogs croaked in a pond none too far away. The moonless sky outside was swarming with stars. They seemed bigger and brighter than the stars that shone over Hyderabad or Toronto. And Sirius the Dog Star glittered like the Kohinoor.

* * *

The old grandfather clock downstairs cleared its throat and gave tongue to six peals. Rajesh awoke wondering where on earth he was. He was encased in a grey cocoon, and he could hear a multitude of birds chirping all at once. Adding to the din was a rooster crowing the arrival of a new day.

Somewhere, a pail was dropped with a clatter; elsewhere, a door closed with a thud. Far away, a dog barked; close at hand somebody laughed. Suddenly among these humdrum noises he heard what sounded like bombs going off in the distance.

Rajesh parted the grey mosquito nets and looked at the window. Day was already beginning to break. The sky was ink-blue with washes of pink and purple. It was the morning of Diwali and people had already begun to burn firecrackers.

He climbed out of the bed, slipped his feet into a pair of flip-flops and walked down to the washroom at the end of the passageway. Later, he took the narrow, winding staircase to the ground floor. The dining room was deserted but beyond, in the kitchen, he could hear the sounds that accompany hectic household activity. The heady aroma of freshly ground south Indian coffee wafted into the room.

As if on cue, Sailu, a helper in the kitchen, popped into the dining room and asked with a wide smile, "Coffee, saar?"

"That'll be great."

Sailu returned to the kitchen and reappeared in a jiffy with a stainless-steel tumbler and offered it to Rajesh. Taking the hot tumbler gingerly by its rim, Rajesh went out into the verandah. He sat on a wickerwork chair, cupping the glass with his hands, drinking in the beauty of the morning along with the sounds and the smells of an Indian village.

"Good morning," Rajesh heard Anil say. Rajesh turned. Anil too had a tumbler of coffee in his hand. He had had his bath already and was dressed in a cream-coloured silk kurta and pyjamas.

"So, you found your way to the dining room. Good," Anil said.

"Yes. It's nice, sitting here in the open, and having coffee."

They could hear fireworks going off, some close by, some far away. Anil sat down on a chair next to Rajesh.

"Breakfast will be served soon. Friends and relatives will be dropping by all morning. In the evening we'll have a pooja," Anil said. "After that, almost everyone, especially the children, will start burning crackers. There will be so much noise, believe me, you'll think you're in the middle of a war zone."

"Sounds interesting," Rajesh said with a smile.

"But until then it's going to be pretty dull. But I'll try to think of something for us to do."

"Don't bother. In fact, I could do with some rest. Seriously," Rajesh said.

But being a good host, Anil did think of something to do to while away that lazy, golden, autumnal day. But for what transpired then, dull was the last word one would choose to use.

* * *

They were seated in the drawing room, feeling full and lethargic. Rajesh had enjoyed the breakfast of a stack of rice pancakes with cocoanut relish and lentil sauce. The house reeked of flowers and frankincense. Streamers of chrysanthemum and mango leaves were stretched across doorways, giving the house a festive look. All through the morning, visitors streamed in to greet the family. Some of them came bearing trays of sweets and savouries. Mrs. Rao or one of the maids would take the trays, and return them, heaped with delicacies prepared in the house.

Kamala came into the drawing room carrying steaming cups of coffee on a tray. She went around the room offering coffee to the guests. She had a woebegone look on her face. It was so uncharacteristic of her that it prompted one of the guests to ask, "What's the matter Kamalamma? You don't look your usual self. Why do you look so sad?"

Kamala did not answer, but a thick voice said, "That's because her husband is home for Diwali." It was Kanna, he had materialized out of nowhere in his trademark fashion.

"One would think it should make her happy!"

"Not if he is a useless fellow like Ramulu. We had not seen him for years. I don't know what made him come back —like a bad penny," Kanna said.

Noticing that Rajesh was getting bored of sitting and doing nothing, Anil said, "Let's go out and do some shooting. We'll take some rifles with us."

"You are kidding, aren't you?"

"No, I mean it. We'll do some target practice."

"Do you think it's safe? I've never handled a real rifle in my life before."

"No worries! It's never too late to learn. It's not a big deal."

They went up to a large strong cupboard at the far end of the drawing room. Anil unlocked it to reveal a selection of rifles arrayed against the back wall.

"Most of these guns belonged to my grandfather. He was a keen shikaari. You would've seen the trophies of animals shot by him. Nowadays of course hunting animals is out of fashion. And anyway, the few wild animals left in the country are protected by law."

Between the two of them they carried a pistol, a couple of rifles and boxes of ammunition and went into the yard. Away from the house, in a clearing surrounded by trees of mango and neem, Sailu had already arranged a table and some chairs. A bunch of concentric red and white circles, fading and pockmarked, had been painted on the wall of a disused shed.

Loading the rifles, they took turns firing at the target. Even Sailu took pot shots at the target. Rajesh was surprised to see how good a shot Anil was. Rajesh asked, "Do you do this very often?"

"Not very. But it is good to do it now and then. There are always dacoits moving about in this area. If they know we have firearms, most likely they'll stay clear of the house."

"What are dacoits?" Rajesh asked.

"They are like bandits," Anil said.

"Oh. I thought they were something like coyotes."

"What are coyotes?" It was Anil's turn to ask.

"They are animals of prey."

"I guess they are much the same thing then," Anil said with a laugh.

While Anil was taking aim to shoot, Rajesh noticed a man shamble up and stand some distance away. The man had a vague grin on his face and wore clothes that must have been natty once. He waited until Anil fired the rifle and then said, "Diwali inam, sir."

"Not now. Later, when I go back to the house," Anil said, turning his back.

The man hovered around the place for some time and left, his smile still intact.

"He's Kamalamma's husband. He's just trying his luck. Inam means a gift and as a tradition we distribute small sums of money on Diwali."

"Not a good man," Sailu said, and added a footnote: "Drinks and beats his wife."

Half an hour later a maid brought in a tray laden with a variety of sweetmeats and salty snacks and placed it on the table. Unlike the other servants Rajesh had seen, she seemed to have taken a lot of care in dressing up. Her hair was shining with oil and combed into a tight plait with the help of a red ribbon. She wore her sari in a way that conveyed she was a man's woman. She hung around, talking flirtingly with Sailu. Under his tutelage she even managed to fire a round from the pistol. The recoil made her giggle.

"Lakshmi, you can go now," Anil said, abruptly. The maid went away without saying a word.

"I think I hear the name Lakshmi once too often in the house. I thought Lakshmi was the name of the short, plump maid," Rajesh said.

"As a tradition, maids take the name of Lakshmi. It's to imply that they bring good fortune—Lakshmi is the goddess of wealth, you know—to the house they work in," Anil said.

"We could call it a *maid*-en name, I suppose," Rajesh said. "But isn't that confusing? Especially if you have as many servants as you do?"

"To differentiate between the various Lakshmis, we end up adding prefixes. Like the maid who brought the sweets is called Sanna Lakshmi meaning Thin Lakshmi. The other Lakshmi you spoke about is called Potti Lakshmi or Short Lakshmi," Anil said.

A little later, Anil's uncle Kanna appeared on the scene, seeming to sprout from the earth itself. "I also would like to give it a try, Anil," he said, picking up a rifle. He fired a few rounds but was a very bad marksman. He put down the rifle much to Anil's relief and melted away just as suddenly as he had come.

"My uncle Kanna suffers from autism," Anil said. "They didn't know it, thirty years ago. They thought it was a spell cast by someone who practises Banamati—you know, black magic, witchcraft."

"Do people still believe in black magic?" Rajesh asked.

"Yes, in remote villages, they still do." Pushing the tray of sweets towards Rajesh, Anil said, "Help yourself."

Rajesh looked at the colourful jumble on the tray and picked up a green and white confection with a cherry-like object at the top. While they were nibbling at the snacks, Anil's young cousins suddenly descended upon them all at once like a flock of colourful birds, twittering and chattering. The boys carried toy Diwali pistols and were firing them indiscriminately, adding to the din.

"We want to shoot with real guns," they cried.

"Nothing doing," Anil said. "Go and play Nachurees or whatever."

"Who wants to play Nachurees? It's a girl's game. We want to play cops and robbers," Anand said.

"With real guns," Raju said, who must have been all of six years.

"Leave, now! Sujata, take them away. It's not safe for kids to be hanging around here," Anil said.

"Let's go, kids. We are not wanted here," Sujata said and marched out along with the other children.

"It's almost two now. Would you like to fire a few more rounds?" Anil asked.

"I'm fine," Rajesh said.

Between the three of them, they picked up the rifles and leftover ammunition. On their way to the house, they passed the children who were seated in a ring under a tree. They were clapping their hands and singing.

"Mango, be quick!" one child said.

"Apple, be quick!" another said.

Rajesh and Anil sat down in the cool and dark drawing room while Sailu went into the kitchen. He returned after some time with Short Lakshmi who carried tall, frosty glasses of lime juice on a tray. Only as Rajesh began to take sips of the ice-cold drink did he realize how hot and thirsty he was.

"It tastes divine!" Rajesh said.

"It's good old Nimbupani," Anil said, swirling the clinking ice cubes in the tumbler. "Nothing like it when you are feeling hot."

"I agree. It's better than any cola or lemonade I've ever had."

Anil put down his empty glass and said, "Let's replace the weapons in the cupboard."

As he was putting back the rifles, Anil asked, "Where's the pistol? Did we leave it behind in the garden?"

"I don't know, dora," Sailu said. "Do you want me to go and look for it?"

"No, I'll come with you," Anil said. "It was very careless of me to forget about the pistol."

Just as they were about to leave, an old maid came in with the missing pistol in her hand. She said, "Babu, I found this on the way to my house."

"Balamma, I'm really glad you found it!" Anil said with relief. "I was beginning to get worried. We must have dropped it on our way back."

* * *

Rajesh went up to his room. Despite the large, creaky fan rotating overhead, he felt hot and sweaty. He picked up the book on Scotland Yard and began to read it, lying on the bed. Even as he tried to follow the murderous career of Dr. Crippen, Rajesh fell asleep.

An hour later, Rajesh woke with a start. He heard someone screaming outside in the yard. He went up to the window and looked out. He saw Short Lakshmi running up from the servants' quarters, shouting and beating her mouth.

Rajesh rushed downstairs. A small crowd had already gathered in front of the house. Anil was there with his parents. He gave a weak smile and said, "There's been an accident."

"Is somebody hurt?" Rajesh asked.

"Yeah."

"Have you called for a doctor? I'm trained in CPR. If you need help, let me know."

"Don't bother. We've called the police."

"Police!"

"Yes, the man is dead," Anil said coolly, in the manner of the very rich who are accustomed to controlling the environment they live in. "It looks as though he has been murdered."

* * *

The police jeep swept into the drive, dragging a halo of dust behind it. The inspector got out of the passenger side of the jeep. He was dressed in crisp khaki and wore brick red shoes. Half a dozen of his minions spilled out of the jeep.

"Good afternoon, Rao-garu," the inspector said, a tall, slim, strong, good-looking man in his thirties. "I'm Circle Inspector Sharookh Hussain."

"Good afternoon, CI-garu," Mr. Rao said.

"I'm sorry to hear that there has been an accident," Inspector Hussain said.

"Yes. It appears that the husband of one of our servants has been fatally wounded."

"Very sad, very sad," Inspector Hussain said. "Did he live in the huts at the bottom of the compound?"

"No, he lived there long ago. Now he lives somewhere in the city. He just dropped by out of nowhere before the festival."

"I see. Could you take me to the place where the crime occurred?"

"Of course, please come along," Mr. Rao said, beckoning them.

Mr. Rao took him away and the clutch of constables followed their inspector like a brood of chickens.

It was some time before Mr. Rao and the policemen returned. Inspector Hussain said, "I've arranged for the body to be taken away for a post-mortem. We'll be sealing the room. From what I could make out, the man was shot to death. Of course, Ramulu is well known to the police. A habitual drunk and a rowdy-sheeter."

"I know, but he was poor Kamalamma's husband," Mr. Rao said. "I wish such a fate had not befallen him, whatever his sins may have been."

"I understand how you feel, Rao-garu." Turning to Anil, Inspector Hussain said, "How's your job in the city? And who is this young man?"

"This is my colleague Rajesh. He is visiting us for Diwali. He's from Canada," Anil said.

"A foreign national, I see," Inspector Hussain said with good humour. "This puts an entirely new complexion on the case!"

"I trust you aren't thinking that the Canadian government has sent an agent to assassinate Ramulu?" Mr. Rao said, joining in the banter.

"If you had known Ramulu as we did, Rao-garu, you wouldn't be saying that!" The inspector turned to Anil and said, "Your father was telling me that you and your friend here were playing with firearms this afternoon."

Anil cleared his throat and said, "Not playing. We were doing target practice in the garden."

"Tell me about the firearms you used," Inspector Hussain said.

"We used two Enfield 303 rifles and a Browning .22 pistol. We spent a couple of hours shooting. When we returned, we realized that we had not brought back the pistol," Anil said.

"You should be more responsible," Inspector Hussain said, shaking his head, "when you're handling firearms."

"We were about to go back to look for it when Balamma came in carrying the pistol. She said that she found it on her way to the servants' quarters," Anil said.

"Rao-garu," Inspector Hussain said, turning to Mr. Rao, "I trust you have a licence for all the firearms in the house?"

"Certainly, for every single one of them."

"Good. I hope you don't mind if we look at all the guns and ammunition you have?" Inspector Hussain asked.

"Not in the least."

"O, Vatsalam!" the inspector shouted, startling everyone around him.

Police Constable Bhakta Vatsalam shot into the room and, his potbelly notwithstanding, smartly saluted his superior.

"This is Vatsalam, my assistant," Inspector Hussain said. "He'll take inventory of the gun cupboard. I'll go back and make arrangements to move the body for the post-mortem. We will be taking fingerprints of some of the servants and the young men here. I hope you'll not mind, Rao-garu," Inspector Hussain said.

"Well, inspector, you must do your duty," Mr. Rao said. "The sooner you clear this up, the better it is for us."

* * *

When it grew dark, the house was lit up as usual for Diwali, but Mrs. Rao had given instructions to tone down the other festivities. She had also forbidden the children from firing crackers that evening.

An ambulance came from the district headquarters to carry away Ramulu's body. As an infant, his doting mother would have suckled him; as a toddler, his admiring father would have held his hand as he took his first wobbly steps; as a young man, his merry-making friends would have clinked glasses with him. But today, rejected by his wife, ignored by his daughter, and only wanted by the police, there was no one to keep Ramulu company. Nobody to mourn him, nobody to miss him.

As the vehicle crawled out of the compound, the light from hundreds of lamps lit its path. The fireworks going off in the village sounded like a gun salute. Notwithstanding the way Inspector Hussain had described him, it could be said of Ramulu that nothing became his life like the leaving of it.

But Kanna, standing in a shadowed corner near the main door of the house, said loudly in his thick voice, for all the world to hear, "Good riddance to bad rubbish. They say Diwali celebrates the triumph of good over evil. How true!"

* * *

The next morning, having had their breakfast, they were all in the drawing room watching a Telugu song-and-dance routine on TV when Inspector Hussain turned up with Vatsalam.

"Would you mind, Rao-garu, if I interrogate the servants somewhere in the house? It would be much better than hauling them off to the police station," Inspector Hussain said.

"I don't mind at all. Treat this house as ... er ... your police station, Sharookh," Mr. Rao said.

"Thank you, Rao-garu."

Sailu and Vatsalam moved a table and a few chairs into a corner of the vast living room so that Inspector Hussain could establish a temporary office there. Anil and Rajesh were the first people Inspector Hussain wanted to speak to. Wearing a very solemn expression on his face, the inspector sat at the writing table. He had a memo pad open in front of him and a pen in his hand. Vatsalam stood next to him like a cupbearer.

"Please sit down. Tell me in detail of what you did and what you saw from the time you went into the orchard for shooting," Inspector Hussain said.

Anil and Rajesh sat down on the chairs in front of the writing table. Sailu stood like a bodyguard behind them. Anil said, "It was about eleven-thirty in the morning when we carried the two rifles and a pistol into the garden near the old shed."

"Who was there with you?"

"My friend Rajesh, here, and Sailu."

"OK. Please continue with your story."

"We were there 'till about two o'clock."

"Were the three of you there all through?" Inspector Hussain asked. Switching to Telugu, he said, "Sailu, did you for any reason leave the place?"

"No, saar," Sailu said.

"Did anyone drop in while you'll were firing the weapons?"

"First Ramulu came, asking for inam."

"What time was it? And how long was he there?" Inspector Hussain said.

"He came around noon. He was there for about five or ten minutes," Anil said. "Thin Lakshmi brought us some snacks at half past twelve. She was there for about fifteen minutes. She also fired from the pistol, only once though."

"Our very own Annie Oakley! What else?"

"Kanna-uncle turned up around one-fifteen, I think. He was there for about ten minutes."

"Go on," Inspector Hussain said.

"At about one-forty-five my cousins came. They hung around for about five minutes. At two o'clock, we collected the rifles and the ammunition and left. We went into the house and had a cool drink. Later, when I was replacing the guns, I realized that we had not brought the pistol with us," Anil said.

"At what time was it?" Inspector Hussain asked.

"I'm not sure, it must have been ..."

"It was around two-thirty pm. Because I remember seeing the time on the grandfather clock in the hallway," Rajesh said.

"When we were about to go back, Balamma came in with the pistol saying she had found it on her way to the servants' quarters," Anil said.

"From what I understand, you don't know when exactly the pistol went missing, am I right?" Inspector Hussain said.

"Yes," Anil said.

"I'm just trying to get the timelines right," Inspector Hussain said. "Later on, both of you will be required to sign a statement. By the way, Mr. Rajesh, when are you planning to go back to your country?"

"You needn't worry. I'll be here for at least two more years, until my contract expires," Rajesh said.

"That's good. I hope your contract doesn't expire as suddenly as Ramulu did!" Inspector Hussain said, shutting his memo book.

Anil and Rajesh got up and walked over to the other end of the room and sat down on the sofa. Though the distance between them and the inspector's table provided a token sense of privacy, Rajesh, who was most interested in the proceeding, could watch and hear without seeming to be eavesdropping.

Having been rounded up by Vatsalam, the three maid-servants trooped into the room. They stood in front of the table like three Graces of varying size and age. The first person to be interrogated was Short Lakshmi. She had wrapped the palloo of her sari around her shoulders and was clutching its corner tightly with one hand. She was almost in tears and kept dabbing her mouth with the corner of her palloo.

"What's your name?" Inspector Hussain asked.

"La-Lakshmi," she replied.

"Where do you stay?"

"In the ser-servants' qua-quarters."

"Stop sniffling, we're not going throw you into the prison," Inspector Hussain said. Then he added as an after-thought, "Not if you're innocent."

The policeman's remarks made Short Lakshmi sniffle even more.

"What were you doing between eleven o'clock in the morning and three?" Inspector Hussain asked.

"I was working," she said.

"Very helpful," Vatsalam remarked.

"Vatsalam!" Inspector Hussain said. He turned to Lakshmi and said, "What were you doing? Tell me in detail."

"I washed the vessels, sir. Later, I helped in the kitchen."

"Go on."

"Then we had lunch and later we made wicks for the lamps from cotton wool."

"Who all were making the wicks?"

"All of us. Myself, Thin Lakshmi, Balamma, and Kamalamma."

"After that?"

"We went home," Short Lakshmi said.

"What time was it?"

"It was just after three o'clock," she said.

"How do you know?"

"I heard the clock."

"From eleven to three did you ever go to the servants' quarters?"

"No."

"Did you see anyone going to the servants' quarters?"

"N-no," she said, and turned to look at Thin Lakshmi.

"I'm asking you again, did you see anyone going towards the servants' quarters?" Inspector Hussain said.

"You can't see the servants' quarters from the kitchen windows."

"I know. But you can from the backyard. Did you see anyone?"

Short Lakshmi spoke slowly, "When I went to pluck some curry leaves from the backyard, I saw Thin Lakshmi going to the quarters."

"What time was it?"

"It was around one-thirty," Short Lakshmi said.

Inspector Hussain made a note in his memo book. Turning to the next maid next in the row, he asked, "Your name?"

"Sanna Lakshmi," said Thin Lakshmi, patting her hair.

"I don't want your description. What's the name given to you by your parents?"

"Jaya Prada," she said, rubbing down a wrinkle on her sari.

Vatsalam barked at her, "Are you being funny? Soon you'll be laughing from the other side of your mouth." Jaya Prada was the name of one of the most beautiful stars of Hindi and Telugu cinema.

"It's true, saar. That's name I was given."

"So, what were you doing between eleven and three pm?" Inspector Hussain asked.

"I soaked the clothes in soap water to wash them later. Then I helped in the kitchen. Amma wanted me to take snacks to the place where Anil-babu and his friend were playing with guns. When I came back, I washed all the clothes and hung them up to dry in the backyard. After that we had lunch," she said, as if she was trained in the art of providing witness statements.

"I heard that you also used the guns?" Inspector Hussain said.

Balamma gasped while Short Lakshmi looked at her namesake with unconcealed admiration.

"Only once, saar. Sailu showed me how to shoot."

"What did you do after you had your lunch?" Inspector Hussain asked.

"Later, we made cotton wicks," she said, with crushing bathos.

"At what time did you go to the servants' quarters?"

Thin Lakshmi was silent.

Inspector Hussain said, "Tell me the truth, when did you go to the servants' quarters?"

"I started to walk towards the quarters but changed my mind."

"Lying to the police is a serious offence," Vatsalam said. "We have ways and means of finding out the truth. If you aren't careful, you'll find yourself in jail very soon."

"OK, OK ... I did go to the quarters," Thin Lakshmi said.

"What time was it?"

"It was just after one o'clock, I think," she said.

"Short Lakshmi here says it was half past one when she saw you walking towards the quarters," Inspector Hussain said.

"I'm not sure now. I had only heard the clock strike one, but I couldn't see it."

Inspector Hussain made a jotting in his memo book. Raising his head, he said, "Why did you go to the quarters, by the way?"

Thin Lakshmi was silent.

"To make cotton wicks, perhaps?" Vatsalam said sarcastically.

Thin Lakshmi glared at him.

"Why did you go?" Inspector Hussain said again, hard.

"My sari had come loose. There were all these young men in the house. So, I went to the quarters to adjust my sari," she said, a shade pleased with her own inventiveness.

"Did you meet Ramulu there?" Inspector Hussain asked.

"Perhaps he helped you adjust your sari?" Vatsalam suggested.

"That's enough, Vatsalam. Lakshmi, listen to me carefully. It is always the best policy to speak the truth to the police. I'll let you go now, but I must warn you, your interrogation is far from over," Inspector Hussain said.

It was Balamma's turn next. More of a Fury than a Grace, she was a tall, strong woman in her seventies and wore an ancient pair of thick bifocals.

"Name?" Inspector Hussain asked.

"Old Lakshmi," Vatsalam said.

"Vatsalam!" Inspector Hussain said.

"Balamma," the old maid said.

"Where do you live?" Inspector Hussain asked.

"In the quarters, next to Kamala's room," she said, as if baiting them.

"How long have you been working here?" Inspector Hussain asked.

"I don't know. But trust me, I started work here before you were even born."

"Don't talk too much. The inspector will throw you in prison, and you'll never see daylight again," Vatsalam said.

"Really? I'm a freedom fighter's wife. Not even the might of the British Empire could deter us. And you think you can put me in a prison, do you?"

"Peace, please!" Inspector Hussain cut in hastily. "Just tell me what you were doing between eleven and three pm yesterday."

"First, I cleaned the rice grains and lentils, and then I chopped vegetables. Later I helped Amma with the cooking. Afterwards Kamala and I set the table. When all the guests had had their lunch, Kamala and I cleared the dining table. After that all we servants had our lunch." Balamma paused to catch her breath.

"What did you do next?"

"Then we sat down to make cotton wicks. Some time after two o'clock, I felt tired. I had come to work early in the morning because it was Diwali. I wrapped the sweets given by Amma in a newspaper, and started to go back to my room," she said.

"Did you ever go the quarters before that?"

"No."

"How did you happen to find the pistol?" Inspector Hussain asked.

"As I was telling you, I left the house around two-thirty. I was walking towards the quarters when I spotted a gun lying under a bush. I thought it was a toy dropped by the children, at first. I bent down and picked it up. But it was so heavy and at once I knew that it had come from the cupboard in the house. So, I went back and returned it to Anil-babu."

"When you left the house, did you hear any sound of a gunshot?" Inspector Hussain asked.

"I can't say. All through the day people were firing crackers and guns and whatnot."

"Did you see or meet anyone coming back from the quarters?"

"No. Other than the children running about, I saw no one."

Inspector Hussain, making notes in his book, said, "All of you can go now. Vatsalam, I'd like to speak to Kamalamma."

The three maids melted away silently, while Vatsalam went in search of Kamala. He returned in the company of Mrs. Rao and Kamalamma. A scrawny child of six or seven, in a faded pink frock which was tomato red in its heyday, was sticking to her side.

"Please take a seat, madam," Inspector Hussain said.

While Mrs. Rao sat down, Kamala continued to stand.

"Sit down, Kamala," Mrs. Rao said.

Kamala hesitantly sat down on the vacant chair, parking her bottom at the edge. She put her arm around the shoulders of her daughter who was standing by her side.

"I know you are going through a hard time. But I wanted to ask you a few questions ..." Inspector Hussain began to say.

"It's OK. Ask your questions, Cl-garu," Kamala said.

"Did your husband have enemies? Do you know of anyone who held grudges against him?" Inspector Hussain asked.

"Some policemen you are! As far as I know, there wasn't a single person in the world that liked him," she said.

"OK, OK," Inspector Hussain said, changing tack. "When did you last see your husband?"

"When they took him away in the ambulance."

"No, I meant, when did you last see him alive?'

"He came to the kitchen in the morning. I went to talk to him. As usual, he wanted money. But I said I didn't have any with me. He wanted me to take a loan from Amma. I said Amma was busy right now and I would talk to her later," Kamala said.

"Can you remember what time it was?" Inspector Hussain asked.

"It must have been about eleven o'clock in the morning," Kamala said.

"Did you ever go to your room between eleven and three o'clock?"

"No."

"Tell me all that happened after you all left the house to go to your room," Inspector Hussain said.

"We finished our work at three o'clock. Short Lakshmi and I started walking towards the servants' quarters. When I entered my room, I saw him sprawled on the floor. There was a lot of blood. I came out and shouted for help."

"Kamalamma, we want to go through your husband's belongings. Would you like to be there when we do it?"

"No, you can go ahead."

"That's all for now," Inspector Hussain said, shutting his memo book. "And thanks a lot for your time, Mrs. Rao"

"Don't mention it, CI-garu," Mrs. Rao said, rising from the chair.

As it was getting late, Inspector Hussain picked up his belongings and took his leave, promising, quite unnecessarily, to return soon to continue with his investigation.

* * *

It was mid-afternoon and Rajesh had already packed his bags. He joined Anil and his parents in the drawing room. They were discussing the murder investigation, while waiting for the jeep to return from the town where it had gone for minor repairs.

"The case will drag on for months and months," Anil's mother said. "It will be a wonder if they ever catch the murderer."

"Do you think I'll have to make frequent visits to the courthouse as a witness?" Rajesh asked, worried by the thought of getting caught in the coils of the Indian legal system.

"You need not have any concerns on that account," Mr. Rao said. "I know the higher-ups in the police department quite well. I'll take care of it."

They heard a jeep come up the drive and stop in the portico.

"I'll go up and get my bags," Rajesh said.

"That's not our jeep," Anil said.

Inspector Hussain, along with Vatsalam, came in.

"Good afternoon, Rao-garu. I'm sorry to barge in like this," said Inspector Hussain.

"You're always welcome, Inspector. Think of this house as ... your camp office."

"Thank you, Rao-garu. I'd talk to you about a couple of points. When the autopsy was conducted, some things of interest were found in the dead man's pockets," Inspector Hussain said.

"What were they, Sharookh, these things of interest? I can hardly contain my curiosity," Mr. Rao said.

"Firstly, there was this small black diary. It contained lists of abbreviations with numbers against them. There was one such list for every month," Inspector Hussain said.

"His monthly expenses perhaps," Mr. Rao said.

"More likely his monthly income. We believe he was blackmailing people. We had always suspected that he was into it," Inspector Hussain said.

"You'd know better."

"Even more interesting, I found this ... this necklace." From a large envelope, the inspector pulled out a photograph with an air of a conjuror. It was a grainy picture of a long chain of gold, strung with coin-like rosettes. Rajesh noticed the look of surprise on every face.

"The photo is bad, of course," Inspector Hussain said.

"My mother has such a kaasumala, Sharookh. She's not here now, she has gone to Bangalore for a visit. But I can check with her."

"In Kamalamma's house we discovered a suitcase with its lock forced open," Inspector Hussain said. "It is too expensive a piece of jewellery for Kamalamma or Ramulu to have in their possession. I just wanted to check with you, that's all."

"I don't know how Ramulu came to have that necklace with him. But I'm sure of one thing: Kamalamma is not a thief. Her forefathers have worked on our farm for generations. Besides, Kamalamma grew up in our house. When she was a child, she used to play with my younger brothers as if she were a sibling. Anyway, if she wanted anything, she had only to ask my mother and she would have given it to her."

"In my opinion ..." Mrs. Rao entered the discussion. "My mother-in-law gave the necklace to Kamala, I remember her telling me that she wanted to give the chain as a gift to Kamala when her daughter was born but was concerned that Ramulu would snatch it away from her. She must have given it to her after Ramulu moved out."

Inserting the photograph back into the envelope, Inspector Hussain said, "Funny thing about this case, Rao-garu, there are so many people in the house but at the crucial time nobody seems to have seen or heard anything. I don't have any eye-witnesses at all."

At that moment, Anil's young cousins entered the room laughing and chatting loudly among themselves. They stopped in their tracks when they saw the policemen.

"Children, why don't you go out and play?" Mr. Rao said.

"We want to see a real detective in action," Anand said. "We're tired of seeing Sujata going about as if she is one of the Five Find-Outers."

"That's enough, Anand. Police-uncle does not want to be disturbed," Mrs. Rao said.

"Let's go, guys. We are not wanted here," Sujata said, and all the children trooped out of the room.

Inspector Hussain continued, as if there had been no interruption. "To cap it all, so many persons in the house handled firearms on that day."

"Isn't it possible that someone came in from outside?" Mr. Rao said. "Saw the pistol lying on the table and took his chance? For one thing, Ramulu had no shortage of enemies. And for another, the gate to our compound is always open. Villagers and visitors keep popping in and out all through the day."

"Yes, it's possible of course," Inspector Hussain said.

"Well, I'm sure you will catch your murderer," Mr. Rao said.

"I have to, I have no choice! I'm expecting a promotion at the end of the year. I don't want to have an unsolved case against my name at this point of time," Inspector Hussain said.

"If I were you, I wouldn't worry, Sharookh. I was talking to your DGP. He happens to be my brother-in-law's first cousin. He was telling me that you are one of the rising stars of the department. And I told him how understanding you've been with this case."

"Thank you, Rao-garu. I'm much obliged," Inspector Hussain said. "I must get going. As you know, the Minister of Education is visiting a nearby village next week to open a new school building. I must oversee the security arrangements. But I'll be back tomorrow, if you don't mind. There are a couple of people I want to talk to."

"You are always welcome, Sharookh," Mr. Rao said. "But I thought you had finished grilling all the suspects."

"I don't have any suspects as of now, Rao-garu. I'm merely gathering information. But I want to question Kamala about the necklace. And I'd like to speak to Kanna."

"Kanna? He's a mentally challenged person. Of what help can he be?"

"It's possible that he might have seen or heard something without realizing its true implication," Inspector Hussain said.

"If I were you, I wouldn't take the trouble. Thanks to his condition, Kanna's not a reliable witness at all."

"You have a point there, Rao-garu," Inspector Hussain said as he rose to leave.

They heard a vehicle come up the drive. It stopped in the portico, and the driver sounded the horn like a flourish of trumpets.

"I'll go and fetch my bags," Rajesh said, and went up to his bedroom. The window was open, and he heard the police jeep drive away, crunching over the gravel drive. A minute later, he heard Sujatha's loud, commanding officer's voice.

"Let's start," she said. "Nachurees, ten rupees, will you please ..."

Rajesh noticed that he had left his copy of *India Today* on the bedside table. He picked it up and stuffed it into his bag. He could hear the children's voices in the garden, clear and loud as a temple bell.

"... name some murderers," Sujata said, getting into the spirit of things. "Such as Jack the Ripper, be quick!"

"Auto Shankar, be quick!" Pushpa said.

"Boston Strangler, be quick!" Anand said.

As Rajesh slid the zipper, it jammed. He had to tweak the slider before the bag closed properly.

In the garden, he heard little Raju, as usual, say, "Err ..."

"Come on say, something, slow coach!" Anand said.

"Give us the name of a killer, or you'll get a D!" Pushpa said.

"Hmm ... Uncle Kanna, be quick!"

Dreams of Gods and Men

"Wake up, Seenu. You must go to work today."

He heard Narsamma speak as if from a far away world. He moved his limbs and opened his eyes. Seenu felt so weak he wanted to sink back into sleep.

The paper-thin mattress he was lying on was the only piece of furniture in the room. No windows, only a small concrete grille under the fluted asbestos roof. The only other furnishing was a gorgeous but out-of-date calendar hanging on a wall. At odds with the gloom all around, it depicted a scene of breathtaking loveliness: a brilliant aquamarine lake framed on two sides by stately pines. In the distance, a snow-capped mountain was brooding over its own reflection in the water.

The calendar had been given to him when Navin Chandra, the sales manager, was clearing his office space after he had resigned from his job. Seenu had helped him pack his personal items into cardboard boxes they got from the factory warehouse.

Two weeks had passed since Seenu fell ill. But the fever showed no signs of letting up, even though he was religiously taking the tablets prescribed by the government doctor. If Seenu didn't report to work soon, he could lose his job. At the very thought of his workplace a bout of anxiety seized him. If he was fired, what would happen to his mother and sister who he had left behind in their village?

"Go to work and see how you feel. Who knows? Seeing how ill you are, your supervisor might give you a few more days off," Narsamma said. A hefty middle-aged woman, she was no relative of his but a do-gooder in his shantytown who could always be relied upon to help anyone in need. She had stopped by with some tea and food.

Seenu rose unsteadily, and then staggered to the neighbourhood bore-well. Though almost fifteen, he was small for his age. He had to pump the handle like a demon to coax out just half a pail of water.

After freshening himself, he drank some of the oversweet, tepid tea which Narsamma had brought for him in a chipped china cup. He left for work, taking a lacklustre aluminum tiffin box which contained his lunch: a dry chapathi and a piece of lime pickle.

On his way to the factory on foot, he was joined by his young colleagues who also worked as labourers in the same factory. They were noisily cheerful, like a flock of sparrows. They were all in their teens, lanky as if they had been cobbled together with only skin and bones, and absolutely no flesh at all.

"How are you feeling?" his friend Ramu asked. "You don't look well."

Plodding silently beside them, Seenu felt too tired to reply.

"I wanted to come and see you. But we've been working overtime for the past week. Some big shot is visiting the factory," Ramu said.

"The supervisor is very angry with you for not coming to work," Prakash, another of his friends, chipped in. "I told him you were not well, but he didn't look convinced."

When they reached the factory gates, Seenu was already out of breath. His legs felt leaden. The boys flashed their IDs at the turnstile. The beefy, macho-mustachioed security guard, who was reading a newspaper, merely emitted a grunt. Sometimes, for no reason at all, he'd box their ears and bark, "Hurry! Hurry!"

At his work spot, Seenu went about his job trying to look busy and energetic. He hoped the supervisor wouldn't come his way anytime soon. But that was not to be.

The supervisor spotted him right away, and narrowing his eyes, bore down on him, his red-tasselled kolhapuris going slap-slap on the cement floor. He was nattily dressed—a blue-striped shirt tucked into a pair of navy trousers. He wore a broad, black leather belt with metal studs and a shiny buckle almost as large as a policeman's badge one saw in American films.

"Why did you come to work, laat sahib?" he said. "You should have stayed in your bed like a maharajah."

"I am ill," Seenu said. He added, putting his palm on his head, "God promise."

"If you are ill, why don't you go home? You will not be fit to do any work."

"No! No! I'm fine, now."

"Look at the broom you are carrying," the supervisor said, grimacing at the stumpy switch Seenu was holding. "Go to the stores department and get yourself a new broom. Do a good job, OK? A very important visitor is expected today."

Seenu hoisted a cheery smile onto his lips and infused some vigour into his walk even though every cell in his body felt otherwise. The issue clerk exchanged the old broom for a new one without asking Seenu a single question. The visitor must be a real VIP! *I'd better be alert*, Seenu told himself. If the supervisor didn't like his work, he'd surely get a scolding. And that was only if he was lucky. Otherwise, it could well be a sound thrashing.

Being beaten by older, stronger people had become a part of his life. As unavoidable as catching a cold in the rainy season or failing in his school exams. One evening, after being caned by his habitually drunk father, Seenu had left his village for good. His father had objected to Seenu going to school instead of working as a farm labourer and bringing home money. His eyes blinded by tears, Seenu had headed to the small railway station nearby, and boarded the first train that stopped there.

Cleaning the floor around the furnace was the hardest part. The area was unbearably hot and always dirty. You couldn't leave the place even for a glass of water. If Seenu was found missing even for a moment, he'd have hell to pay. The more he swept, the more waste the furnace seemed to throw up. No matter how much he cleaned, the place always looked grimy.

Seenu ran into Jagan, an office boy, who was walking briskly across the shop floor. He had a sheaf of papers in his hand. He stopped by to talk to Seenu.

"Haven't seen you for ages. How have you been?"

"I'm OK. There's a lot of cleaning to do today. I heard a special visitor is coming."

"Yes, from the World Bank. I had better hurry."

How Seenu envied the office boys. They wore company-issued uniforms and worked in cool, sweet-smelling environs. In Seenu's eyes, they had the best job in the world. To get that much-coveted job, you should at least be able to read and write elementary English, even if you couldn't speak it fluently. If one of the office boys didn't come to work, sometimes the cleaning staff were asked to help. Seenu got the chance to work in the office a few times. How paradisaical it was! No grime on the floor, no back-breaking work, mostly taking papers from one table to another, and serving endless rounds of tea.

On one such occasion, he had met Navin-sir. They'd chatted as Seenu helped him pack his stuff. Navin-sir was leaving not just the company but the country too as he was emigrating to a country called Canada.

"Where's Canada?" Seenu had asked. For a moment he had presumed it was the province where people spoke Kannada, a language not very dissimilar to his mother tongue of Telugu.

"It's half a world away. It's near America."

Everybody had heard of America. He had seen American films. They were filled with half-nude women, criminals and policemen.

"Is it easy to go and live there? Is it better than our country?" Seenu asked.

"It's not easy to move to Canada. You need a passport and visa to go there. But it's far easier than moving to countries like England or Germany. Canada is a beautiful country. Basic education and healthcare are free there. It helps if you have a college degree and can speak English." He handed over the calendar, which he had hung on a wall in his cubicle, to Seenu.

"These are scenes from Canada," he said. The calendar had outlived its purpose as there was no need now for Navin-sir to enjoy Canadian natural beauty vicariously. "As you can see, it can be very cold out there in the winter."

The landscapes of Canada were very impressive. Though the drifts of snow shown on the last two pages were a bit unsettling. But Seenu was more struck with the idea of free medical care and education: the two things which impacted him and his family more than anything else.

Seenu made up his mind to move to Canada. One day. He would educate himself and learn to speak English. To hell with Canadian winters.

* * *

Seenu often recalled the night he arrived in Secunderabad station after leaving his home, without a paisa in his pocket, without even a clue as to what he'd do next. The passengers trickled out of the various coaches and made their way to the main exit, forming a surging river of humanity. Seenu had followed at its tail end until he found himself deposited outside the station. The crowd disintegrated all at once, leaving him behind like a piece of driftwood.

It was late in the night. The glare of city lights and the blare of horns confused and scared Seenu. He stood outside the station for a long time not knowing what to do. He made small forays into the city streets, which looked sickly and grimy under the yellow streetlights. In the end, he scampered back into the station which somehow seemed familiar—throbbing with life even in the middle of the night.

The next morning, completely unnerved, he tried to find a train that would take him back. The numerous tracks and platforms baffled him. He sat down on a bench, feeling lost and forlorn.

Then suddenly, a gang of boys descended upon him like a host of sooty angels. They were the children of the street. They did odd jobs in and around the station for a living. They lived on pavements, in derelict buildings, or in a shelter nearby. The children plied him with numerous questions as if they were the CID. Maybe, convinced of his bona fides they took him under their wings. That night Seenu accompanied some of the children to a night shelter and was introduced to the warden. In exchange for attending a prayer meeting and listening to the warden's uplifting sermon, Seenu received a light supper and a bedroll to sleep on for the night.

Soon, hopping into trains and hopping out of them became Seenu's daily routine. Learning quickly how to avoid the ticket collector's slaps, he earned good money sweeping the floors of the railway coaches. He would crawl crab-like, with a piece of rag in his hand, cleaning the floor, and collecting the coins flung at him by grateful passengers.

He thought of his mother and sister every now and then, wondering how they were coping. But he was happy that he didn't have to attend the village school and get beaten by his schoolmaster for not answering the questions or not doing his homework. And how he had hated exams!

Every year they would turn up like some annual scourge—
like dengue or chicken gunya.

But it wasn't as though he could entirely escape getting
beaten in the city. Sometimes he was picked up by the police, thrashed and then released for no apparent reason.
Sometimes the older boys roughed him up if he did not part
with some of his income, however measly. But somehow life
went on; days spent on clattering trains, and nights in the
shelter, on a rooftop or under a staircase.

That was until one day Ramu said, casual-like, that Raj
Kumar, one of their friends, had got himself a job in a factory. A factory! All of them had snickered—what a come-
down from trains. But one evening, when they ran into Raj
Kumar, they got the shock of their lives. He was dressed in
modish clothes. He wore Rayban sunglasses and had Adidas
on his feet (even if they were counterfeit). He had always
been a little snooty, and now he gave himself even more
airs. He spoke of Employee State Insurance and Provident
Fund and God-knows-what-else. Raj Kumar admitted that
his uncle knew a contractor who hired workers for offices
and factories. Were they interested?

"I can always put in a word," Raj Kumar had said loftily.

They didn't believe him one bit. But one day, on Raj
Kumar's advice, Seenu went to meet the contractor. The
man was pot-bellied, and a wreath of grey-black hair ringed
his bald, oily skull. He wore a different gemstone ring on
each finger as lucky charms. A chain of rosary-like beads
hung from his neck, and he had holy ash smeared on his
forehead. He surveyed Seenu from head to toe and said,
"Who sent you?"

"Raj Kumar."

"The film actor?"

"N-No," Seenu said, rattled by the contractor's way of speaking. "He's a boy, like me. You got him a job."

"Oh ... Prabhakar Rao's nephew?"

"I-I think so," Seenu said, even though he had no idea whatsoever.

"Have you also come for a job?" He stifled a yawn.

"Yes."

"You'll have to talk to my supervisor," he said, and then shouted at the open doorway, "Arre, Appa Rao!"

Seenu was startled, but a man walked into the room. He was slim and of medium height. A faint grimace was pasted on his mouth, like a price sticker that couldn't be peeled off.

"Sethji of Bhavani Metals has asked me to increase their housekeeping staff," the contractor said. "They are going in for ISO certification. He wants the factory to look very clean. See if this boy is suitable."

The supervisor in turn appraised Seenu keenly as if he was studying Seenu's bone structure through some sort of X-ray vision he had. Without a word he turned his back, but as he was walking away, he said, "Follow me."

A surprised Seenu scurried after the man, tailing him into a small room whose walls were lined with filing cabinets, steel cupboards and posters on workplace safety. The man sat down on a chair behind a table that had all kinds of files and papers heaped on it. He said, "What's your name?"

"D. Srinivas."

"How far have you studied?"

"Seventh class."

"You think you can get a job having studied only up to seventh grade? The streets are full of double MAs who are looking for work. What's your age?"

Seenu, being forewarned, lied. "Seventeen."

"You don't look a day more than twelve. You had better put on some weight. You can't be too careful with these labour officers. I don't have any vacancies right now. If anything turns up, I'll let you know."

On Raj Kumar's advice, Seenu petitioned the supervisor week after week. The supervisor pretended to be annoyed but didn't seem to mind at all. He seemed to enjoy the importance people like Seenu gave him. Seenu couldn't remember how many times he had visited the supervisor at his office, but one day, the supervisor said, "Be here tomorrow at seven o'clock in the morning. There's a job available in Sethji's factory. I'll show you the place."

The factory siren stood in for the engine whistle, and to sweep the factory floor he was given a long-handled broom—a decided improvement on the piece of rag he used to carry. But there was no comforting rumble of wheels under his feet. Who cared? This was not like the permanent job his friend Raj Kumar held in a multinational manufacturing plant, but the moolah came in once a month when Seenu proudly scrawled his signature on a flesh-pink revenue stamp next to his name. So, from morning to evening he worked his broom, sweeping the shop floors, sweeping the toilets, sweeping this, and sweeping that. You wouldn't believe how many surfaces there were that needed sweeping.

He even began to put aside money so that he could give it to his mother. On an occasional weekend, he would jump onto a train—tracks and platforms didn't confuse him anymore—and go to his village. His mother never failed to say, "How lucky we are. Thanks to you, now we can save for Lacchi's dowry."

He always made a point of leaving before his father returned from the toddy shop. But on his last visit, less than a year since he started work at the factory, Seenu came to know that his father had passed away the previous month. His mother looked frail and helpless. She was neck-deep in debt because she had borrowed money for his father's funeral. And she herself needed money for the many ailments the village quack kept diagnosing her with. His sister had been sent to a far away town to work as a servant for an upper-class family who hailed from their village. God willing, she would marry and settle down if they could save enough for a dowry. Or else she would end up as one of the women who eked out a living walking the street.

* * *

Seenu swept the floor in right earnest, but with every passing minute, he grew more and more tired. Returning to work before he was fully recovered was a mistake. But what could he do? The money he had saved for his sister's wedding was now being spent on buying medicines for his mother. Age, overwork and malnutrition had taken their toll on her, and the village doctor—a charlatan—discovered a new disease in her no sooner than the old one was cured.

The supervisor, with a frown plastered on his brow like a Hindu holy mark, appeared amid the heat and dust of the furnace room.

"Meera-ma'am wants to see you. What have you done this time? You're always causing me trouble."

Seenu did not know what slip-up he was supposed to have committed; he had just returned to work after a fortnight's absence. With a quaking heart, Seenu went into the admin building. Meera-ma'am was boiling with rage, anger overflowing like lava from her glowering eyes. On seeing him she started ranting. "What did you do with the letter for Krishna Kumar-sir? Sethji wanted immediate action on it. Now Krishna Kumar-sir says he doesn't know anything about it."

"You said it was for Krishna Murthy-sir, so I left it on his table," Seenu said, stammering. Though it happened nearly a month earlier, he recollected taking the sheet of paper and rushing to Mr. Krishna Murthy's cabin. As usual, he was not at his seat. Seenu placed the document on his table under a globular glass paperweight with colourful entrails.

"Krishna Murthy? You fool! I clearly remember saying it's for Krishna Kumar. Why do you make my life so difficult?" She added rudely: "Wait here!"

Meera-ma'am slipped into Sethji's chamber. After a couple of minutes, the door opened and Meera-ma'am poked her head out and said, "Sethji wants to speak to you."

Seenu was seized with indescribable terror as he entered the holy-of-holies. The room was very cold, the polar chill caused as much by the manically humming window AC as Sethji's cold-eyed glare. Sitting grim-faced behind a large glass-topped table, he looked like an unbenevolent god.

"You bloody idiot! You leave important documents any-where and everywhere it pleases you!"

In reply, Seenu managed to croak, "On K-K-Krishna Murthy's ..."

"Can you even begin to guess how much financial loss you've caused me? Useless fellow! Get out of my sight!" Sethji said, his indifferent eyes turning to a computer monitor.

Meera-ma'am lead him out. Seenu had nearly passed water in utter fear. Meera-ma'am said, "You can go now. Tell your supervisor to meet me."

With those ominous words ringing in his ears, Seenu left the admin building. In the event, three days' pay was docked from his wages. This time round he had had a nar-row escape. Seenu realized that the next time he wouldn't get a second chance.

* * *

During the lunch break that followed the keening of the siren, Seenu remained silent while all the contract workers were laughing and jabbering around him.

The last time he went to his village, his mother had said, "How lucky we are. If you didn't have such a good job in the city, what would happen to us?"

What if he was thrown out of the job? What should he do? Go back to begging on trains? Living off the train was fun while it lasted, but how much money could he put aside?

The chapathi he had brought tasted like sandpaper, and the pickle had all but lost its savour. The only time in his life he got to eat a square meal was when he lived in the shelter. One evening, while the impatient boys sat cross-legged on the floor, their empty stomachs rumbling like a train rushing over a bridge, the warden, a gentle, unfocused-looking old man who was always mixing up their names, spoke about the world being only an illusion, it was all part of Brahma the creator-god's dream. Once the god woke up, the universe would—poof!—cease to exist.

Could that be true? Seenu had pinched himself. It hurt. His body bore many a testimony to physical pain. Life didn't seem to be anybody's dream. The warden must be batty. But how did it matter? At least he was kind.

The siren wailed again, and the labourers rose from the bare floor they were sitting on, dusting their backsides. They trooped solemnly back to their respective stations, leaving their camaraderie behind like belongings in a left-luggage office.

"Look sharp," Prakash said to Seenu. "The bigwigs will be visiting your area any time now."

The area around the furnace felt hotter than usual. Sweat broke out all over Seenu's body. The metallic fumes from the furnace brought on waves of nausea. His head was throbbing, and he began to shiver despite the heat. Though he felt hopelessly weak, he desperately tried to put more vigour into his work. He had three more areas to clean. Would he have the strength to last?

In the distance Seenu saw Sethji making rounds in the company of important-looking men dressed in dark suits. Seenu panicked, but the regal trio moved away in another direction. Heaving a sigh, he let his body relax.

He continued to sweep the grubby floors with as much energy as he could muster. But he reached a point where he just couldn't go on. The heat both within and without was proving too much for him. As if in a dream he limped to a quiet corner, away from the busy workmen and their mindlessly shuttling forklifts. He sat down to recoup his strength. The picture in the calendar came to his mind. How cool and pleasant a place it must be! He wished he could live there. A wave of intense lethargy stole over him, even as he imagined walking along the shore of the shimmering lake, breathing in the crisp mountain air. But before he realized, sleep overcame him.

He didn't know how long he had dozed off but through a fog of drowsiness he heard people walking around, murmuring. He tried to shake himself awake and get up. But sleep—deep, delicious sleep—pulled him back into its soft, comforting folds.

Seenu woke suddenly when he was rudely shaken and physically lifted. It was the supervisor holding him by the collar, his face empurpled with anger. Without a word the supervisor punched Seenu in the stomach, sending him sprawling. Seenu fell like a rag doll on a heap of scrapped machinery lying in a corner.

"Stupid fellow! You were having a nice nap when Sethji came along with his guests to the shop floor. And the place was so dirty! It looked as if it hadn't been swept for years." The supervisor gave a sob, and then screamed, "I'll lose my job because of you! You bastard! I should have thrown you out ages ago."

He tugged at his belt so roughly that a belt loop of his trousers broke. The belt uncoiled like a snake. The supervisor flailed at Seenu even as he lay supine on the small hill made of discarded metal parts. Seenu raised a feeble hand to ward off the whiplashes. The supervisor beat Seenu until

his aching arm forced him to stop. He threw the belt on
Seenu's face, kicked him, and strode away.

Seenu was too weak even to push aside the belt. The
broken pieces of machinery bit into his flesh. But the misery which welled in his heart made him indifferent to the
pain racking his body.

The sweat on his brow shone like morning dew in the
glow of the furnace. His boyish face looked like that of an
angel as he drifted slowly into sleep. He felt his body relax
and the fever ebb away. If the world was Brahma's dream,
what would his nightmare be like?

A tiny smile lit up his face as he tipped over into a
dreamless sleep.

A Portrait of My Mother

My mother died several years ago. Yet, I feel her presence around me often. A supportive and beneficent presence in times of need and in times of excess. Like a stake holding up an enervated sapling, in good weather and bad. A clumsy metaphor perhaps, but I was never good at expressing my thoughts. I feel Mother's influence even now as I write; her small warm smile, full of understanding, goading me on.

I know what you're thinking: here's a cuckoo if ever there was one! Think what you may, but I do need moral support. Alone and lonely in this big bad world, I can do with some help. Help from any quarter, and who better than your own mother? Even if she's dead and gone?

I don't blame people who think I have a screw loose. Poor ignorant souls. What do they know of everlasting love, a love that transcends time and space? People don't call me a nutcase to my face. Thank goodness for small mercies. Anyway, it doesn't stop them from saying and doing things behind my back: looking at each other meaningfully, rolling

their eyes, shaking their heads, rotating their forefinger
near their temples.

If only they knew!

* * *

When I first got the news from India of Mother's death, I
was living in Canada, having moved there as a student a
few years earlier. I was working as an admin clerk in a firm
that supplied bathroom fittings. Mother had been very insistent that I sally forth into the world and make the most
of any opportunity that came my way. Even if it meant I left
Mother behind, alone and lonely.

"Alone, yes. But not lonely. Loneliness is a state of mind,"
Mother had said.

When I got a letter of acceptance from a Canadian college to do a post-graduate program in International
Development, the triumphal joy one felt on such occasions
was tinged with nervousness and self-doubt. Mother said,
"Kiran, you must learn to live independently. You can't hang
on to my apron strings forever. And I am not going to live
forever, either."

"Mother, don't speak like that!" I may have sounded a
trifle melodramatic, but the exclamation was literally
wrenched out me by some atavistic fear.

"Death is not the end," Mother said as if she was spout-
ing some Hindu philosophical mumbo-jumbo. "My bless-
ings will always be with you whether you are in India or
Canada." Mother could give a Bollywood songwriter a good
run for his money.

"Canada is so far away! The winter there must be so
unbearably cold!"

"It takes as much time to fly to Toronto as it takes to go by train to Kolkata. Of all the developed countries, Canada, I am told, is the most welcoming of immigrants. You'll get used to the cold, as you've got used to the summer heat here. Besides, it is a lot safer."

Safer! It wasn't for nothing that safety mattered so much to us. My father had died in the infamous terrorist attack called the Mumbai Blasts. It had happened when I was a mere toddler. Besides the grief of bereavement, Mother must have felt scared, even terrified, of the uncertain future staring at us. Mother was a homemaker, unqualified in any way to find a job. We ended up subsisting on the goodwill of relatives, my father's pension, and the ex-gratia the government doled out to the kin of victims of calamities. The government's largesse wasn't a humongous sum, and the monthly pension's value, small to begin with, was continually eroded by inflation over time.

As for terrorist activities, they continued to flourish, occurring with seasonal regularity in different parts of the country—nay, in different parts of the world. The papers and the TV channels were bringing news of terrorist plots, wars, natural disasters, and accidents into our living room. So much so that it became Mother's one-point agenda to pack me off to a safe haven.

Poor Mother! Despite all her hopes and efforts, I too was destined for a brush with terrorism.

* * *

Mother's body was discovered by the servant maid who came to work at the crack of dawn. When there was no response to her insistent ringing of the doorbell, the maid

woke the neighbours and alerted them. When the front
door to the apartment was broken open, they found Mother
lying prostrate on the ground. Pain inerasably frozen on her
face, her right arm was stretched towards the phone table,
a pretty brass and teakwood affair.

Was she trying to call me when she felt the onset of a
stroke? In India there is no 911 you can reach out to. Only
your family and friends, sometimes even foes, if you ever
needed help. But what practical assistance could I have
given her, living as I did on the other side of the planet?

I left the same evening for home, paying the exorbitant
last-minute fare by dipping into my overdraft account. No
journey ever seemed longer. I was alternately crying, sleeping and dreaming. Dreams, I've noticed, never seem to have
a sense of occasion. Waking up groggily and gradually from
a dream in such circumstances was one of the most heart-
piercing feelings you will ever experience in your life.

It was still dark when the plane arrived at its destination, but rather than landing, it hovered exasperatingly over
the airport. It was as though the pilot was testing the waters before he made the decision to dive. In the east, touches
of red were bleeding into the overarching blackness. Even
the day looked bruised. My patience was wearing thin, but
at last good sense seemed to have prevailed and the aircraft
made its descent.

After collecting my scant luggage and passing through
customs, I came out of the airport, and joined yet another
queue, this time for a taxi. As we passed street after street,
the city was waking up from a restless sleep, gradually spilling people onto the sidewalks, and vehicles onto the roads.
There was a grimy feel to the air and the cityscape looked

as if it could do with some serious scrubbing. Even in my bereavement, I was reacting like a typical émigré, ungrateful and insensitive.

One thing to say for death, it attracts people like flies. People known and unknown to me had gathered in our apartment. Jet-lagged and bewildered, I allowed the priest, hastily hired for the occasion, to hijack my life for the next few days. I went through the motions of the funeral rites, all as ordained by the scriptures, like an automaton.

The one point about the ceremony that left a lasting impression in my memory was the moment I lit the funeral pyre. I was strictly enjoined to stand with my back to Mother's body and extend my hand—which held a flaming torch—backwards to set fire to the kindling. But when I was carrying out the instructions, involuntarily I turned around and stole a glimpse of Mother. She looked like a helpless ragdoll on the bed of misshapen logs.

By glancing over my shoulder, I had done the unthinkable. I had neglected to leave the dead behind once and for all and make a clean break with the past. A collective groan, as palpable as smoke, rose from the onlookers in the crematorium.

I stayed back for a month to wind up my affairs. The apartment had been mortgaged years ago to pay for my study abroad. There were some interesting pieces of furniture, carry-overs from more prosperous times, but the one keepsake I wanted take back with me could be found nowhere. It was a portrait of my mother. It was done years ago by a painter-friend of my father, Siva-something-or-the-other, who later in life became a celebrity, with even Sotheby's and Christie's auctioning his works for astronomical prices.

Though the portrait was not a realistic and careful study (it had clouds of unexpected colours, and lines which didn't go all the way home), Mother looked alluringly lovely. The masterful portrait, in a magical way, captured her youthful exuberance. The picture had originally hung in a prominent place in the living room, drawing 'oohs' and 'ahhs' from visitors. But after my father's death, his grim-faced photo-studio portrait had the pride of place. Mother moved her portrait to an inner room, which acted as an improvised study, a nook where I did my homework, and Mother attended to her correspondence and filed important documents.

Mother's portrait had a unique aspect that fascinated me when I was growing up. Her eyes seemed to follow you all over the room. Wherever you stood, her unwavering gaze was always directed at you. As a child I would walk in a zig-zag manner and turn around again and again to catch her looking elsewhere. But no, her eyes were always fastened on me.

The maid had no knowledge of the whereabouts of the painting. Servants kept changing and the present help had been employed for only a few years. The portrait must have been stolen by an opportunistic thief or sold by my indigent mother. There was nothing I could do other than swallow my disappointment.

Bargain hunters and used furniture dealers arrived on cue and carted away whatever had resale value. I gave away the crockery and cutlery (there was no dearth of them) to the maid and other menial staff who worked in the apartment block.

On the day I was to head back to Canada, I stood in the eerily empty living room with a collection of outsized bags around me. Stripped of all furniture and furnishings, the room looked unfamiliar and unappetizing. I was waiting for the kindly neighbour who offered to drive me to the airport. When the doorbell rang, I turned around and gave the apartment a final once-over. I was engulfed by an indescribable feeling of loneliness.

* * *

The psychologist, Dr. Dotti, asked, "Key-ran, how exactly do you feel your mother's presence?"

It was the office manager at my workplace who suggested I consult a psychologist. The services were on the house as the employee health insurance paid for it. So, I decided to give it a try. I had been experiencing bouts of depression which was affecting my work and attendance.

But the psychologist, far from dealing with my melancholia, cottoned onto the bit about Mother.

How was I to answer Dr. Dotti's question? You'd know, wouldn't you, when you were in the presence of your own mother? The very air seemed to carry Mother's love like a fragrance. The haunting smell of the perfume she wore mixed with her own body odour. The scent of love.

Dr. Dotti persisted, "Do you hear her? Do you see her?"

"No! No!" I said emphatically. Voices in the head! Apparitions in the night! She could as well have accused me of being insane. Or possessed. Perhaps, already convinced of my peculiar condition, she was only trying to figure out which of the two.

"Then how does your mother ... manifest her presence?" My bizarre affliction could make anyone struggle for words.

"I don't see or hear anything. I just feel her presence."
Like the cool shade of an oak tree on a hot afternoon. The
shade is not a solid three-dimensional object but despite its
insubstantiality you can find so much solace there. But at
that moment, I couldn't articulate my thoughts—I never
could in those days—so I remained silent.

The psychologist simply wouldn't let things be. I'm certain she must have been a Gestapo officer in her previous
life. "You mean, you just become aware of her. Like your
internal radar picking up something?"

"My mother's not an enemy aircraft!" I said with asperity.

"I'm sorry, I didn't mean to put it that way. It's only that
I want to get a better grip on your condition."

I knew then and there that the consultation wouldn't
do me any good other than sow seeds of doubt and confusion in me. I clammed up but pretended to go along. After a
few more equally fruitless sessions, the meagre amount the
insurance policy paid ran out.

"Key-ran, we were making such remarkable progress, I
wish you would continue with your sessions," Dr. Dotti said,
in a voice laden with disappointment.

Of course, she would! Regarding her disappointment, I
wasn't sure if it stemmed from losing the small but steady
source of income or for letting loose an untreated psycho on
the city streets.

* * *

It was not in fitness of things for a person who had academic
training in International Development to peddle plumbing
materials. But what could an immigrant do?

For a start, look for a better, more meaningful job. Which was what I did, however unrealistic the ambition. To my surprise and pleasure, I landed a position in a not-for-profit organization that provided drinking water and sanitation facilities to impoverished communities in Asia and Africa. The intimate knowledge I possessed of bathroom fittings must have had something to do with my success. Yes, something, but not all. I gave most of the credit to Mother's overseeing presence, encouraging me and inspiring me, as always.

By and by I grew to be more confident about myself and the bouts of depression were becoming things of the past. I threw myself into my new job, heart and soul. I became more focused, and it showed in my performance. My new boss liked my work and said so in as many words.

An opening came up in one of our field stations in Botswana. I applied for the posting. As I hailed from a Commonwealth country, the initial two-week orientation program in England was the main draw for me. London! The ground zero of the empire upon which the sun had never set! The city's very place names conjured up visions of power and glory: Buckingham Palace! Westminster Abbey! Tower Bridge! The city was the setting for many of Dickens' novels, which I was force-fed, even if in abridged avatars, when I was young by my school and Mother. Despite doing well in the interview—I was a past master of plumbing, after all—I did not make the cut. I was extremely dis-appointed. I even felt that Mother had let me down.

It was only later I was to realize how wrong I was about Mother!

Whenever I ran into Maryann, the person who snagged the foreign posting, I felt envious. She looked pleased as punch. How I wished I was in her shoes. I hoped someday I too could clinch a foreign posting and bask in the feeling of success as Maryann obviously did.

Two weeks before the date of departure for London, Maryann came down with shingles. Since I was the only unattached person, a person with no family or friends to tie me down, I was prepared to travel abroad at short notice. I felt ecstatic and sent up my thanks to Mother, who I thought had pulled strings from the place above.

Before you could say, "Jack Robinson!" I was on a plane to the Big Smoke in economy class. In London, I went to the training school, and lived parsimoniously on the measly allowance I was given. But I felt a high I had never done before in my life.

On a day off I started early so I could savour the touch and feel of London to its fullest. It was the seventh of July and I can recall the day as clearly as if it was yesterday—as would many Londoners. When I left my flea-bag lodgings I had no specific plan in mind. I just wanted to be footloose and fancy-free. After getting off the tube, I walked aimlessly, absorbing the atmosphere of London, a bustling, sparkling mega-metropolis—as long as it didn't rain, of course. At around nine am, I took the bus number 30 at Marble Arch. It was an impulsive decision. I was close to the bus stand when the bus rolled in. I ran up and boarded the bus on a whim, just to experience a ride on the iconic red double-decker; so much like its colonial cousin in Mumbai, only shinier, fancier and less crowded.

I sat in a window seat right in front on the upper deck, unaware that it would be the epicentre of the carnage which followed. I divvied my time between gazing out of the front window and peering out of the one to my left. I wanted to make the best use of the fare I had paid. London, in all it's enchanting beauty, either unfurled in front of me or sped past like a series of postcards. What a nice and economical way to see London. As Mother would say, cheap and best.

I knew not then that the double-decker was trundling inexorably to its doom.

At Euston Station, many passengers got in. Downstairs, there was much talking—so unusual and heightened that the murmurings wafted up. But I didn't care. This was my first and probably only visit to London and I didn't want to be sidetracked for any reason.

The bus gave a lurch and moved on, making its stately if leisurely progress. But you can enjoy the sights of London only so much from a regular bus. Just a procession of shops, though many of them looked swanky. Whoever said England was a country of shopkeepers was dead-right. Window-gazing was beginning to pall when suddenly I was blind-sided by a sight which shook me.

There, in a store window, I caught sight of Mother's long-lost portrait in all it's glory. It was just a glimpse as the bus lumbered past a long stretch lined with shops, but there was no mistaking it. I was part excited, part puzzled. How could Mother's portrait have landed here in London of all places? Without giving it too much thought I leapt up, rang the bell, and, picking up my knapsack, rushed to the stair-well. When I came down, the bus was slowing down to a halt at a bus stop.

I jumped out and retraced the way to the shop where I thought I had spotted the painting. It must have been about a hundred or two hundred metres up the road. When I reached the approximate point, I couldn't find any art shop or studio. There were the usual dreary ones, like convenience stores, coffee shops, pharmacists, and such like. I paced up and down the street but found no trace of my mother's portrait, or anything remotely resembling a painting. There was only one shop with a prominent storefront. It was an apparel shop. In the window there were a handful of stylized, unhuman looking mannequins sporting the latest in summer wear. The store appeared almost deserted. I hesitated at the entrance. Surely this couldn't be the shop which had displayed Mother's portrait?

When I heard a muffled explosion in the distance, I didn't immediately think of a bomb, despite my personal history. However, people ran out of the shops around me, including from the one I was planning to enter.

"Another one has gone off," somebody said, looking down the road. I, too, turned in that direction and saw a wispy column of black smoke rise and make for the sky. The same man added: "What's the bloody world coming to?"

"The bomb appears to have exploded on the road itself!" someone else remarked.

"In a car, perhaps?" yet another suggested.

I walked into the store which was now devoid of any customers. There was a harried looking woman in a dress suit shouting instructions to another woman who soon disappeared behind a back door marked 'Staff Only.'

The woman turned to look at me in a distracted manner, her mind obviously on other things. Her body language messaged her impatience.

I said, "I am looking for a portrait ..."

"What portrait?" she said, puckering her brow.

The world around us erupted with the clamour of multiple sirens. Police cars were making a beeline presumably to the place marked explosion.

"A portrait of my mother," I said, over the din. "I thought I saw it in your shop window."

"We don't sell paintings. We are a garment shop. Now if you will excuse me, I am about to shut the shop."

I was turning to leave, when the other woman reappeared from the back room.

"The bomb was in a double-decker bus! Dozens have been injured."

"Dear me!" said the woman in the dress suit. "Sarah, you'd better get a move on if you want to make it home safely."

"Goodbye," I said to the women. "I too must get going. Have a nice day, ladies."

"Nice day, indeed! You look new to the country. I hope you are not using the public transit? Bombs have been going off on trains and buses," the woman in the dress suit said.

"You needn't worry," I said with uncharacteristic decisiveness. "My mother is always looking out for me. Her eyes follow me wherever I go."

The woman stared at me with her mouth open, forgetting for a moment the London bombings.

Dancing on the Beach

T he beach is deserted. Desolate dunes rise and fall like
gigantic waves. The sky is grey and cheerless, the water,
cold and uninviting. At the horizon, heaven and earth have
indistinguishably become one.

Hoping to sort out her thoughts, she has been trudging
along the shore for nearly a mile. She can hear the strains
of distant music over the bedlam in her head. The music is
so soft that it seems to emanate from another world. Yet,
the music is more palpable than her immediate surroundings: the painful sand underfoot, the unruly waves slapping
the shore, the trees swaying in the wind. Growing in volume, the music takes complete hold of her, overshadowing
the bitter, disjointed thoughts whirling in her mind.

Thoughts of Adi and his Mamma.

The beat of the music acquires an exhilarating ur-
gency, prompting her to break into a run. She leaps about,
kicking up clouds of dust. The concerns weighing on her
mind begin to melt and drift away. Prancing and pirouet-
ting, she begins to dance with a never-before-felt abandon.

An intense joy suffuses her being, and her heart wants to lift anchor and float away.

* * *

Adi's breakfast sputtered in the pan. Sorry-looking chicken sausage, pulpy, penial. Only chicken was permitted in the house now. Thanks to Mamma and her sensibilities, other meats were banned. An unbreachable embargo.

She had woken up at quarter to six, even before the alarm rang. It was still dark outside, and sleep dogged her as she shuffled about the kitchen. Adi worked as a dispatcher in a trucking company, so he had to get to work early. The breakfast she rustled up at such an ungodly hour was invariably slapdash. What else could anyone expect? Anyone but Mamma. She always felt that her son was being shortchanged. Why couldn't she get out of her bed and make something delectable for her son?

My poor son. What can I do? I'm too old and sickly to cook for him.

But even her age and health didn't stop her from being an indefatigable busybody. To be fair, she didn't talk much, lacking fluency in English as likely as not. But Mamma could make her opinion known with her eyes, nose and brow. The unspoken comments were as clear and conspicuous as italicized words or bold font.

Mamma was a new import from back home. After her husband's untimely death by cardiac arrest, Mamma packed her suitcases and moved to Canada. Along with her money bags, a cool half-a-million, give or take a thousand. In Canadian funds, too. Not rupees. Mamma didn't have to jump through hoops to wrangle a visa. Bank statements were the best passports.

Three years ago, Adi and she had met at a party thrown by their mutual friend. They were both international students. They hailed from the same town in their home country, so for some unfathomable reason they thought this made them allies in an alien land. They began dating, and a few weeks later, they started sleeping together, and before the year was up, they were married. A tragedy—or was it a comedy?—in three acts.

Adi was of medium build, just shy of being puny. He was good looking, though not in a jock kind of way. What had impressed her was his gentleness of speech, and his attractive smile. What had he seen in her? She was short and unshapely. She drank, smoked, and tended to put on weight if she didn't watch. A gregarious and fun-loving person, she had a habit of laughing loudly at both opportune and inopportune moments. "A free spirit" was the phrase she liked to use to describe herself. Very different from the sort of young women he may have known back home. Especially his older sister. To an undeservedly lucky young man his sister made a dream wife: a pretty thing on his elbow at a party, a responsible mother to his children, a chef in the kitchen, a whore in bed, a servant maid everywhere else. And all unpaid at that.

What was Mamma's take on her daughter-in-law? No prizes for guessing:

A nightmare, if I may say. A most unsuitable match. A marriage made in Hell.

Their marriage had seemed great at first. In those stressful, uncertain times, waiting for the PR card, searching for a job, Adi and she were like kindred spirits. They were of support to each other and took a special delight in being together. To her, life appeared wonderful, like a fairy tale. Especially when compared to her life back home, dominated by an alcoholic father and a stepmother wholly preoccupied with her own children. But after the unheralded arrival of you-know-who, their happy camaraderie began to come unstuck.

The urge to smoke jangled her nerves. She resisted the temptation to fetch her packet from her handbag. Anyways, she couldn't have lit up right away.

"You can't smoke in the house. What will Mamma think?" Adi had said.

One restriction after another was imposed on her. She had tried to push back, but Adi had pleaded with her to try and understand his plight. He was the only son and was duty-bound to take care of his mother. Besides, there was the matter of inheritance. Poor Adi. He had the unenviable responsibility of walking the tightrope that spanned two opposing cultures.

Now she was bound in chains. Only the leg irons remained to be clamped on.

There was a slight tremor in her hands. Her head hurt. She had one too many last night. If Mamma came to know, she would blow a gasket. Since they stopped having drinks at home, Adi and she had gone out under the pretext of an office party.

They seem to be partying all the time ... What kind of job is it?

Mamma was correct to wonder. Her niggardly employer, a buy-now-pay-later furniture store, treated its employees to dinner only once a year for Christmas at a Chinese buffet. Cheap. Like the furniture they sold. How she hated going to work there! But she must. It was a lifesaver. It took her away from the house for the better part of a day.

She packed Adi's lunch, leftovers from last week. She never claimed to be a cordon bleu cook, and Adi didn't seem to mind her slipshod efforts all these months. But of late, he'd been bringing back his lunch half-eaten. Missing Mamma's touch?

Poor boy. He doesn't get good food to eat. Look how much weight he has lost!

Get your damn mother to cook for you!

Adi had said, "You must understand. Mamma had servants back home."

She has one here, too, pumpkin. Unpaid, at that.

Adi came into the kitchen, which meant Mamma had woken up. She must be sitting on the recliner in the living room, all bundled up in shawls though the winter was long past. She was waiting for her morning cuppa.

"Have you made tea?" Adi asked.

"No. Make it yourself."

"Let's not start all over again."

"Who's starting? Can't you see I'm making sandwiches?"

Adi made tea for himself and Mamma. Only loose leaf, no teabags for the old bag. After all, Mamma had the moneybags. What bags did she have? Only the ones under her eyes.

When Adi returned to collect his lunch bag and juice box, he made as if to give her a hug. Or a kiss. Both of which were becoming lackadaisical of late. She was holding a spatula in her hand, and though unintended, she must have looked like a fencer holding an epee. Adi backed off, and said, "See you in the evening."

"I'm going out with my girl friends today."

"Not again! You went out with them only a couple of days ago."

"Seven days ago, to be exact. It's Samira's birthday today."

Adi made a face. His mug looked better when he grimaced.

"Don't be too late."

"You can tell your mother I'm held up at the store."

Without saying anything further, Adi left for work. She collapsed into a chair at the breakfast table. She could do with a drink right now. A stiff one.

On many an occasion she wanted to throw in the towel. But she had yielded to the dictates of common sense. Surprising as it may seem, she had a hard, practical side to her personality. It may have had its origins in her insecure childhood. Turning her back on her marriage was easier said than done. Having to live alone once again on foreign soil was a daunting prospect.

Adi had often begged her to have patience. Patience for what? Did he believe it was only a matter of time before Mamma dropped dead? Even with all her ailments—including high cholesterol, high blood sugar, high this, high that—there was fat chance of it happening soon. Immigration had been good for Mamma. There were capable doctors and reliable Medicare here.

She should get going. There was no time to indulge in self-pity. If she didn't hurry, she was going to be late for work. But the thought of recycling the insipid remnants into lunch for herself sickened her. There wasn't enough time to cook anything fresh. She had an appointment with a customer, recently arrived from Saudi Arabia, who claimed he intended to buy a whole lot of furniture and appliances. Maybe if she closed the deal, she could treat herself to a sandwich at the nearby Coffee Time.

After changing into her work clothes, she ran a comb to subdue her recalcitrant hair. Pausing only to grab her handbag and car keys, she rushed out. Outside, it was grey and blustery. She started the car and roared out of the driveway. The traumatized tires squealed as the car turned into the street. In spite of herself, she smiled as she imagined Mamma's irritation at her precipitate if noisy departure.

Words fail me. What an ill-behaved woman! I can't imagine what my son sees in her.

But the smile was short-lived. The fuel light was on in all its glory. Shoot! She needed to fill up before she hit the highway. She should have topped up last night, but she had put it off, procrastinating as usual.

There was a long lineup at the pump. Before she could back out to find another gas station, an SUV crept up behind her and blocked her path of escape. The driver of the car in front, rather than pay with his card, entered the attached store and refused to return. The electronic clock on the dashboard ominously recorded the passage of time, minute by flashing minute. The driver eventually came out, with a coffee cup in hand, armed to face the morning. The entire world was on edge.

After she filled up the car, she headed to the highway. When she glided down the ramp, she saw, with a sinking heart, the sluggish progress in traffic.

Now crouching, now crawling.

She realized with a fatalistic feeling that she would never make it to work in time. She looked for her mobile. As usual it had gone AWOL. She fossicked in her handbag with rising panic before she remembered that she had left it on the hallway console, after calling the customer to reconfirm the appointment.

It was over! She couldn't even call a friendly colleague to sub for her. The store had a shoal of underpaid sales associates circling like sharks to ambush an unwary customer. Especially Omar. Even his teeth were like those of a shark. Any surprise he snagged the largest sales bonus every year?

On the highway, there was no turning back. You went with the flow. She made slow and excruciating progress in stone-faced silence. Her eyes stared ahead, but they were not on the car-crammed highway, not even on the distant horizon.

Ignoring the signs pointing to her exit, she pressed on, putting mile after mile behind her. The road steadily emptied of traffic, as if it had sprung multiple leaks. Nearly an hour later, she took the exit at a point where she knew the road would lead to a lonely beach. Adi and she had chanced upon the place during the random, destination-less jaunts they undertook when they were dating.

She pulled up at a convenient spot near the beach. Stepping out of her car, she decided to take a stroll to becalm the thoughts roiling in her head. The landscape was hopelessly grey but for plucky puccoon shrubs with their smiling blooms. Drops of sunshine in a world of gloom.

* * *

Her dancing is becoming wilder, almost frenetic. The tempo of the music is rising into a crescendo. The music is coming neither from electronic equipment nor from the celestial spheres. It seems to issue from somewhere deep within her.

Savouring the freedom, she wants to banish all thoughts from her mind. Thoughts of home, of Adi, of Mamma, and even of herself.

But it's not to be. Adi's inaction, Mamma's interference, are very hard to let go. Adi the Mamma-worshipper!

She knows she's being both unfair and uncharitable. Adi's as much in a jam as she is. But why does he let things slide? Why can't he take a decisive action one way or another? Or, for that matter, why can't she? What's she waiting for? A divine sign? Get real, girl!

How wonderfully liberating it is to dance on this beach. The wind on her face, The wet sand under her feet. The only things restraining her are her clothes, even if they are noticeably skimpy.

Mamma could never understand her views on dress. Mamma judged her through the prism of propriety she brought like baggage from another culture.

Does anyone from a good family dress like that? Look at the low-cut blouses she wears, showing half of her bosom. And does anyone go to work in such revealing outfits?

She chuckles loudly when she imagines Mamma's scandalized face. It has been ages since she has laughed so heartily. Does Mamma think the clothes she wears are improper? She's right!

She begins to peel of her garments one by one and cast them away. She curvets and cavorts in the buff, uncaring of the elements, uncaring of anything. She has never felt so free before. It's like getting a taste, even if a small lick, of ultimate Nirvana.

She wants the music to continue forever, but it ceases as if someone has pressed the stop button. She comes to a standstill and raises her hands to the sky in supplication. The sky is clearing, revealing patches of blue. Suddenly, the sun breaks through the swathes of clouds, pouring light and warmth upon the landscape.

Her mind made up, she turns around abruptly and re-traces her steps. She bends down every now and then to pick up her discarded clothes.

It's time to pack up and leave.

Noises Off

When we first started hearing the scary sounds in the night, I was seven years old and my younger brother, five. We had recently moved into an independent house with our parents, having lived earlier in a cramped condo. It was before Lili had taken up work as a nanny to take care of my brother and me.

I woke from sleep one night, not knowing what had awakened me. Then I heard it: the soft tap-tap coming from the next room. The empty guest bedroom. The house we had moved into, though new to us, was a very old one. It had a lingering musty smell, having been without occupants for a long time. Daddy had insisted we buy the place because it was a terrific bargain, much to Mummy's displeasure. She thought the rundown house would need extensive repairs and was far away from everything.

The knocking noise coming from the adjacent room continued, sometimes persuasive, sometimes insistent. Who would want to make those sounds in the night? The noise had a crinkly tone like someone was beating a tattoo on a glass pane. It sounded as if someone, or something, was asking to be let in.

Sweating with fear, I lay awake in bed and listened to the sounds. I tried to wake up Dave, my younger brother. To call him a sound sleeper was an understatement. Not even an earthquake could interrupt his slumber.

After much shaking, he opened his sleep-soaked eyes.

"Can you hear it?" I whispered to him.

"Hear what?"

"The tap-tap sound. It's coming from the next room."

He listened incuriously and said, "Who could it be?"

"I don't know."

"A thief?"

"I don't know."

"A ghost?

"I told you I don't know!"

"Why don't you go and see who it is?'

"I'm sacred. Will you come with me?"

"No. I'm sleepy," he said with careless bravado. "Go tell Daddy or Mummy."

Luckily, my parents were home that night. Sometimes we would be left alone, though only for a few hours. My parents often worked in the evenings—my father in a factory and my mother as a nurse—and though they did their best to juggle their schedules, it didn't always work out. My parents were new to the country, so they had to work doubly hard, we were told, to succeed. I, too, was new to this country, for that matter, though I hadn't much recollection of living anywhere else. We were immigrants. We looked different, we ate different, we spoke different. But above all, many had us believe, we smelled different. As if to make up for all this my brother and I were given carefully chosen traditional names which could easily be spelled and pronounced as local names.

I shuffled to their bedroom, knocked on the door, and entered. I flipped on the light.

My mother awakened and asked groggily, "What is it now, Harry?"

I told her about the sounds coming from the guest bedroom.

Daddy, too, woke up, and said with irritation, "They must be the floorboards creaking. This is an old house."

I thought I heard Mummy snort.

"It sounds as if someone's tapping on the window," I said.

"Which burglar in his right mind would knock on a second-floor window?"

"It may not be a burglar ..."

"You don't believe in ghosts, do you?" Daddy said, sneering.

"It must only be a branch of the apple tree hitting against the window in the wind. Now go back to sleep," Mummy said.

Adults! The way they react, they must be a different species altogether. Defeated, I went back to my room. Growing louder, getting nearer, the tap-tapping continued for some time before stopping. But my fear did not disappear immediately, and by the time I finally fell asleep, it must have been early morning.

Night after night, I heard the rapping sounds. The noises, as long as they lasted, kept me frozen in my bed with fear. I didn't get much sleep on most nights. Was it a surprise, then, that I felt drowsy in the classroom and pooped out on the playing fields?

This situation couldn't be allowed to go on for ever! One night I plucked up courage and crept into the neighbouring room to see for myself. Alone, because I couldn't shake off my younger brother's sleep. I barely stepped into the dark room, when the noise started. Tap-tap, tap-tap. Loud and clear, it was like Morse code for "come closer, come closer." The only window was in the far wall, faintly lit up by a distant streetlamp. Then I saw a movement at the window, and the lights outside brightened and then dimmed. I screamed.

I heard footsteps, and Daddy came running into the room. Mummy followed close on his heels. My shriek must have been extremely loud, sleep-shattering if not exactly blood-curdling, because it flushed out even my younger brother from his bed. He rolled in, looking like a sleepwalker.

Daddy switched on the light. The noises had stopped, or my family was making so much din that you couldn't hear them. Daddy moved to the window and opened it. He peeped out and then put his right hand out and scrabbled the air, as if he was trying to shoo away the pesky ghost.

"The apple tree is too far out," he declared.

"There may be raccoons hidden somewhere," Mummy said. She was the one with ideas. "This is an old house."

Her last comment irritated Daddy. "Don't bring it up every time! There are no raccoons living in the house!"

My parents moved Dave and me to a makeshift bedroom in the unfinished basement downstairs. Daddy hired an expert to come and investigate if there were any raccoons freeloading on us. The man found neither raccoons nor ghosts.

Though it cost a packet, a carpenter was induced to come to our remote house and check the windows and fix the screens.

And they hired Lili.

* * *

Lili was in her late twenties. She hailed from our home country, but she had been living and working in Cyprus, the international holding tank for nannies. She was minding three problem children while dreaming of finding a passage to Sweden or Switzerland. When she got the offer of a job in Canada, she took it, telling herself half a loaf is better than no bread. The fact that she was fresh off the boat didn't seem to bother her.

"Everybody's an immigrant in this country," Lili said airily. "Some came a few minutes ago, some a few days ago, some a few years ago, some a few decades ago, some a few millennia ago."

"Not Dave," I said. My younger brother was born here in Humber River Hospital. He's as Canadian as maple syrup, poutine and beaver tails.

"Possibly," Lili said.

* * *

Once Lili entered our lives there was more order. At least initially. She ensured we did our homework and ate on time, feeding us yucky vegetables like carrots, broccoli and spinach. She made us sit in a corner if we indulged in too much mischief. She also made certain that we didn't watch more TV than was good for us. She gave the impression of being one who brooked no nonsense. She was a nanny on a mission.

The good thing was that I stopped hearing the nocturnal sounds. We had moved back to our bedroom and I slept as peacefully as Dave did in the other bed. I didn't know who to thank, the rodent control guy or the window glazier guy or Lili, our autocratic caretaker.

My parents must have spoken to Lili about me hearing noises in the night, so she enquired about it.

"I haven't heard them in a long time," I said. I hoped Lili didn't think I was a weirdo who imagined things.

"That's nice to hear. But what kind of noises were they?"

I told her, feeling even more embarrassed. I neglected to tell her about my scream which had brought the entire household to the haunted room. I had later discovered that what I saw at the window was nothing more than a shadow cast by the headlamps of a moving car.

"What I can't wrap my head around is," Lili said, "who or what would want to knock on an upper window?"

"Somebody very tall?" I suggested.

"Who could be so tall as to reach a first-floor window!" Dave said dismissively.

"Somebody walking on stilts, perhaps," Lili said. She sounded half-serious, almost mocking, as if she was teasing us.

"Somebody who can fly," my little brother said. His teachers had told my parents that young Dave had brains. I wasn't very good at either studies or sports. The only time I distinguished myself in school was when I got a role as a witch when my grade staged a scene from a play by that Shakespeare dude.

Lili took our place in the unfinished basement, sharing space with her two inseparable companions, the washing machine and the clothes dryer. It was unpretty outside, and it was getting colder as fall was already upon us.

"When I become rich, I, too, will have a nice bedroom like your mother's. Nice matching furniture and a lovely vanity table with lots of fancy stuff on it ..." It was true that my parents had a well-appointed bedroom. Mummy had recently snagged a good job, the likes of which didn't usually come a new immigrant's way. While this made her justifiably proud, she still had to work late nights.

Lili added under her breath: "... until then I have to rot here." When she realized I had heard her, she said, "Don't tell your Mummy I said that. She can get very annoyed. Your Daddy's different. He's easygoing."

Lili was both stern and strict with us, with no sense of fun. Or so it seemed to us. Sometimes, when caught off-guard, she would tell us about her home country, which was ours, too, yet the tales sounded so strange they may have been of another planet. She spoke about the hardship, the squalor, and the danger that lurked in every corner. But still, one could detect a sense of ... What was the word starting with the letter N? Nausea? You know, a heart achy longing for the days which have passed?

Otherwise, she only referred to our home country in cautionary tales she concocted only to set us right. Like, "If children misbehaved or were dishonest, they were spirited away by bandits who come in the night," chiding me in a roundabout way because I hadn't brushed my teeth and lied about it.

Lili's favourite pastime, after her duty of minding us was done, was to watch wrestling on TV. After putting us to bed, she would go to the kitchen make herself a mug of hot chocolate and settle herself on the recliner in front of the TV—provided my parents were at work.

Whenever the sounds of the TV (so different from the ominous tap-tap sounds!) woke me in the middle of the night, I'd creep out of our bedroom, and squat on one of the treads of the staircase to watch Lili watching TV. A couple of times, Dave, the champion sleeper, also followed me and settled himself on the step next to me. Even my younger brother was not immune to the charms of late-night television!

"What are you two doing there?" Nannies have eyes at the back of their heads. "You should be in your beds!"

"I heard noises, so I came out to see."

"Harry, you're always hearing noises!"

"I had a bad dream. I ... I'm not getting sleep."

"If you have been bad, you'll get bad dreams. Now be good boys and go back to your beds."

* * *

Winter was around the corner. At Daddy's insistence, Lili was shifted to a spare bedroom upstairs. The small space heater she had close to her narrow bed in the basement would be no match for the approaching Canadian winter. The house we lived in was old and the ancient furnace could barely keep the cold out. From a conversation—more of an argument, really—I overheard, my parents had neither the intention nor the money for any massive makeover. Of late, Mummy and Daddy had started bickering over little things. As days passed, their disagreements became stronger and more frequent.

"They are stressed," Lili said. "There's a big mortgage to pay off. Besides, they work too hard. I wish they took time off to relax and have some fun."

By and by, the atmosphere in the house began to lose its happy feel. As children we did not understand everything, but we could sense the change. The first aroma of a storm brewing.

I was hearing noises again. Not the soft tapping on a windowpane as before. I heard floorboards creak. Sometimes, I would spot a shadow pass in the strip of light under the bedroom door. Sometimes I could even hear moans. Whatever it was, it was now within the house, and had become very bold, making its presence felt, even when Daddy was around.

One evening at homework hour, Lili was going through my answer sheet for a pop quiz. She shook her head in disapproval at my scores. I tried to put the blame on my lack of sleep.

"Are you hearing noises in the night?"

"Yes, now and then," I said, feeling like a fool.

"That's not good," Lili said. "You are a light sleeper. I wish you were more like your younger brother."

"Dave sleeps as if somebody has slipped a mickey into his Milo."

"That's interesting," Lili said. She had a thoughtful expression.

* * *

On another day late in the evening, Lili came to our room. She had a grave face, like she had put on a mask for the occasion.

She said, "You may be right, Harry. I too have started hearing noises. It's like someone prowling in the house."

"See? I've been right all along!" I said. "Maybe we should tell our parents—" Before I could complete my sentence, I was cut off.

"It's no biggie. Our parents know about it already," Dave said.

"Yeah, it's no biggie for you. You can sleep through a tornado!" I said.

"Your brother's right. We needn't tell your parents. It will look as though I'm somehow inefficient. Besides, the thing has been here for a long time. It may not do any harm ... if you remain in your beds. You know what, Harry, I will make a strong tisane for you. It's a special recipe my grandmother, who lived in the mountains, gave me. It will help you sleep better."

I started taking the funny-tasting preparation Lili made for me every night before going to bed. It did help me sleep better, though sometimes I could hear the poltergeist noises as if in a dream. Like the meaningless sounds you hear coming from the stage when the curtain is down.

* * *

A few days later, I found myself being rudely shaken in my bed. I could hear sounds, some near, some far away. My first thought was that our ghost had got me.

When I opened my eyes, my eyelids still heavy with sleep, I saw, up close, Dave's frightened face. Even in my drowsiness I was surprised by the reversal of roles.

"I think the ghost is strangling Lili," he whispered.

I too could hear Lili's moans. Accompanied by other sounds, it was coming from a room farther down the hall.

I'd have preferred to cover my head with the blanket and go back to sleep, but Dave kept egging me on. "Hurry up! We have to save Lili."

I got off the bed and stumbled out of the room. Dave followed me. We went to the room from where the sounds were coming. It was my parent's bedroom. The door was slightly ajar, and I pushed it open. What we saw was a sight somewhat familiar and reassuring. It was no biggie, if I could borrow from my younger brother's vocabulary.

* * *

It was a Monday morning in February, and everyone was at home for the recently introduced Family Day holiday. The morning was bright and crisp, and a gorgeous day had been forecast. How often predictions go wrong, met or otherwise.

We were having breakfast. Daddy was making the most sumptuous omelets, tossing in everything he could find on the kitchen counter. Mummy was making our traditional pancakes on an electric griddle. Lili was in her room. She always made herself scarce when Mummy was around.

Mummy asked me in a matter-of-fact way, just as a conversation filler, "So, Harry, are you still hearing noises in the night?" She had no idea what she was getting into.

"Kinda," I said.

"What do you mean by 'kinda'?" I couldn't tell if Mummy wanted to know more about the noises or she didn't approve of my monosyllabic responses.

"Oh, it was nothing after all," my little brother chimed in, as though he was setting to rest finally all the doubts and contradictions surrounding the nocturnal phenomenon. "It was only Lili and Daddy wrestling in the bedroom."

I could never figure out adults. A frigid silence greeted what I thought was Dave's innocuous comment. But it was just the lull before the storm. Soon, all hell broke loose.

To cut a long story short, it was the last time we had a meal together as one family.

The Mystery of Indira's Hair

I t fell in a sheer ruler-straight drop, and almost reached her waist. When she moved her head, it glinted like the wings of a raven about to take flight. What age-old secrets were used to maintain it, nobody knew for sure. But one thing was certain: no hairdresser's crimping iron or curling tong ever touched a single strand of hair on Indira's head.

What little was known about Indira, whether her hair or her life, came in small driblets to her colleagues. Indira was a relative stranger, a newly landed immigrant who was dumped on them as a volunteer worker. She didn't talk much. Some people, kind and charitable, thought her a taciturn person, while others, ignorant but presumptuous, suspected a lack of fluency of English in her. In truth, her reticence may have been nothing more than a newcomer's desire to keep her counsel and stay clear of controversies. Her clear-cut assignment was to work for free so that she could acquire that most vital requisite: Canadian experience. It was a qualification which recruiting agencies in general were not prepared to overlook in a candidate.

On Indira's first day in the office, Peggy Hardbottom, the office manager, a no-nonsense lady who concealed her thriving grey hair with chestnut-brown dye, made her sign a sheaf of documents. Then the two took the building elevator to the first floor, which housed a Tim Hortons outlet. Peggy bought Indira a double-double, the welcome drink Peggy treated all new employees to, paid or unpaid. Seated at the small table overlooking a parking lot peppered with discarded paper tumblers, hand tissue and excreta of Canadian geese, Peggy sipped her milk-less, sugar-less dark roast and gave Indira a run down on the company business and Indira's role in it for the next three months. Indira listened with her habitually phlegmatic expression, even though her job duties didn't go much beyond filing papers and photocopying documents.

Peggy put Indira through the paces on office etiquette and dress code. Then Peggy rose and, on her way out, dropped her coffee cup into the trash cabinet. Indira faithfully followed suit, even though she hadn't consumed all of her double-double, and trailed after Peggy like a shadow. In the office, Peggy took Indira on a tour, introducing her to all the employees. Indira followed with a smile fixed on her pleasant but tense sienna-brown face. While her smile looked like something she had borrowed for the occasion from an advertisement for toothpaste, there were no two opinions about her glorious, glowing tresses that draped her head like a lustrous mantilla.

The hectic whistle-stop tour, which featured a lot of enthusiastic glad-handing, finally came to an end at a room which appeared to hum with activity. The room contained half a dozen workstations, most of them occupied with women who were busy—busy on the computer, or busy on the phone, or busy perusing files. As Peggy had mentioned, it was the time of the year when work was at its most hectic. It was a period immediately before the deadline, and the public was making desperate last-minute tax-saving investments.

At their entrance, some of the workers suspended their work and looked up. Those who were on the phone returned to their conversations. Peggy conducted Indira to an unoccupied workstation in the room. It was bare and cold, begging for the warmth of human presence. Other workstations were populated with emblems of working life: heaps of files, stacks of documents, handbags and lunch bags, framed photographs of smiling, mostly blond children, bottles of water, and even an opened bag of potato chips.

The lady at the neighbouring workstation removed her headphone and turned to look at them. She smiled and said, "Hello!"

"Sandy," Peggy said. "This is Indy-ra. She is the volunteer I spoke to you about. Indy-ra, you will be working with Sandy. She will tell you what kind of assistance she needs. Sandy is one of our best CSR's. You will enjoy working with her."

"I'm sure," Indira said.

"Welcome to our department," Sandy said to Indira after Peggy left. "We are really in need of help. There's so much work to do,"

Sandy had honey-coloured hair with blond highlights. She had pearly artificial nails at the tips of her fingers. She looked pretty in a way a flower pressed between pages of a book does.

"I'm happy to be of help," Indira said.

The various members of the team introduced themselves over the partitions of their cubes like friendly neighbours do over palisades: Anna, Yasmin, Jane (or was it June?), and Valeria.

Sandy handed Indira a sheaf of documents and said, "Can you have them scanned for me, please?"

Noticing Indira's blank expression, she added: "I'll show you how. Come with me."

Sandy piloted Indira to an alcove around the corner which housed the photocopier/scanning machine. It was the size of a washing machine. She showed Indira how to use it.

"You can send the scanned copies to my email," she said, "until you get your own email address. Would you like to try?"

"Yes, please," Indira said. After a few false starts she got the hang of it.

"You're a fast learner!" Sandy said appreciatively. "Once you're done let me know; I'll give you some more. There are masses of them. I hope you don't get fed up!"

"No problem," Indira said. "I understand you all are overwhelmed with work. I will try to be of as much help as possible."

When Indira finished scanning the copious quantities of documents, she was handed an even bigger batch. After Indira did them, she was given a bunch of checks to be photocopied. Later, she was shown a mountain of papers that had to be sorted and filed in the right folders.

Before Indira knew it, it was lunchtime already.

"Would you like to join us?" Sandy asked.

"I didn't bring a packed lunch from home," Indira said. "I didn't know what the setup would be like."

"Everything must seem new and different to you!" Sandy said.

"There's a vending machine in the kitchen but there's a restaurant on the ground floor of the building," the woman Indira thought was Jane said.

"The restaurant is a bit pricey. Only June can afford to eat there," Sandy said.

Indira picked up her handbag and accompanied her colleagues to the lunchroom. Sandy and June (it *was* June, not Jane) pulled out their boxes from their lunch bags and one after another proceeded to reheat their meals in the microwave.

Indira looked around at the slot machines which hosted a variety of shrink-wrapped, meal-sized foods. Indira peered at the labels: beef sandwiches, veal cutlets, chicken fajitas, pretzels, potato chips, cookies, and so on so forth. She gingerly inserted a two-dollar coin and entered the alphanumeric code for a pair of oatmeal cookies. The packet fell with a thud into the compartment at the bottom to the accompanying merry tinkling of change.

After extricating her purchase, Indira studied the mind-boggling options of the coffee dispenser. She selected French vanilla. When the machine started noisily pissing into the pasteboard cup, her hitherto tense face broke into a smile of intense delight. She had got it right!

As she approached the table, Indira said by way of explanation, "I'm vegetarian."

"Way to go, girl," Sandy said with a smile.

"My cousin is a vegan," June said. "It's always a challenge when she comes over to dinner."

"I know, I find there are few choices for a vegetarian," said Indira.

"How's it in India?" asked Sandy.

"Many Indians are vegetarians, so there are many restaurants that proudly claim they are 'pure vegetarian.'"

"How about work? Is working in an office in India very different?"

"I have never worked in an office environment before. Either in India or Canada."

"What kind of work were you doing in India?" Sandy asked.

Indira paused before saying guardedly, "I worked for a theatre company." She added a wry laugh.

"Bollywood!" said June. "How glitzy."

"So, we have a star in our midst," Sandy said, smiling.

"Not at all," Indira said. "I used to oversee costumes. For a small company that staged plays. It hardly made any money. I got next to nothing as pay."

"It's pretty much the same thing here, eh? I mean, working for free as a volunteer," Sandy said.

"Why do you work if you don't get paid? I'm not going to work without pay for any reason!" June said.

"In Canada, without Canadian experience, it's hard to find employment, so volunteering will help—at least I hope so. In India, I took up the job because theatre was my passion, and any work associated with it, whether it was well-paid or not, gave me pleasure. Besides, I didn't really have to go to work. My husband was an executive in a multinational company which paid its employees well. Here, it's different ..."

The door was roughly kicked open, and a young man entered the kitchen. He had a half-full bottle of water in one hand and a couple of rubber maid containers in the other. He had dirty blond hair and was good-looking and well-built. Young as he was, he exuded an aura of strength and power.

"Hi ladies," he said, throwing a quizzical look at Indira.

"This is Indira, she's a volunteer in our department," Sandy said. "Russell is a hotshot fund manager."

"Hi! Do you like working here?" Russell asked as he proceeded to reheat his food in the microwave.

"Today is her first day, for Chrissakes!" June said.

"I like what little I've seen," Indira said. "It's a new experience for me."

"She's from India," June said like one might say, she suffers from shingles.

"Really? What part of India?" Russell asked, filling up his stylish-looking glass bottle at the water cooler.

"I'm from Bhopal. It's a small city in ... in central India."

"I've visited Delhi, Agra and Mumbai," Russell said.

"Russel has seen almost every country in the world," Sandy said.

"Except Canada," June said.

"That's true," Russell said with a laugh. "For different reasons, I have never stepped out of Ontario."

The microwave beeped and Russell pulled out the big lunch boxes—apparently his appetite was huge in all matters. He left the room, somehow contriving to open the door even though both his hands were full.

When the ladies went back to work, Indira was given another stack of papers—the size of Mt. Everest!—to file. Indira, without grimacing or emitting a groan, began the unexciting task. She was a bit slow but she was giving the documents the due attention before she filed them.

Indira seemed to enjoy working in the office, even if the work she did appeared to be little more than drudgery. If any colleague requested Indira to run office errands, like handing over urgent mail to the receptionist for despatch by courier, she did them cheerfully. She was always pleasant and polite and was willing to help and willing to learn.

"This place is cool, clean, safe, and it has such a nice work atmosphere," Indira said, sounding like a real estate agent when Yasmin asked if she liked working there. She added: "How different it is from the warehouse where I worked earlier! It was stuffy and hot, and I had to move heavy boxes from one place to another. I was always scared that I would sprain my back or get hit by the forklifts that were buzzing around like flies!"

As days passed, Indira ceased to look less and less like an exotic creature. Seeing her day in, day out, her colleagues began to accept her as one of their own—though one with the most remarkable head of hair. On the whole, her colleagues seemed to like Indira, though they found her inscrutable in some ways. Precisely in what ways, it was difficult to pin down. While she was always courteous, she also seemed to be a private person, rarely volunteering to divulge personal information. There was a whiff of mystery around her.

"The better word is mystique," Yasmin said, when they discussed their new colleague amongst themselves.

"She's a nice, hardworking person," Sandy said, "I hope Peggy offers her a full-time job after her three months of volunteer work is done."

"Appearances can be deceptive," June said. "Still waters run deep."

"I won't believe that of Indira!" Anna said. "She's not a very talkative person, but whenever she speaks it has a ring of truth. It doesn't sound phoney."

"Maybe she isn't so excited about her job because we give her the most dull and menial jobs to do," Yasmin said.

That very afternoon, Sandy said to Indira, "I know you must be getting super-bored. We'll see if we can vary your routine a little."

An hour before closing time, Val popped her head mole-like above the wall of her cubicle and asked Indira, "If you're done with filing, would you like to learn how we send out our mail?"

Indira put aside the stack of unfiled papers, which had reduced from a deluge in the early days to a small but steady stream, and followed Val to the mail room. There was a huge automatic franking machine along one wall. Standing opposite to it, there was a rack with large pigeonholes. The compartments were labelled, and they were populated with varying number of envelopes, big and small.

While teaching Indira the intricacies of the franking machine, Val asked, "I hope you don't mind doing this kind of work?"

"Certainly not," Indira said. "I'd like to learn as much as possible. There seems to be so much more than simply licking a stamp and sticking it on an envelope!"

"You're right! And once you know the drill, it isn't very hard."

"Machines are taking over all the jobs," Indira said. "They are faster and cheaper than people."

"Unfortunately, they're better, too. They make fewer mistakes. I heard you went to university. I'm sure you'll find a good job soon."

The door was pushed half-open and a plump woman with blue eyes and a halo of curly yellow hair stuck her head into the room.

Looking at Indira, she said, "I'm Mary from Redemptions."

Indira stared at her and was too startled to say anything. Val laughed, as the door opened further, and Mary stepped into the room.

"Val, you're here, too! I didn't see you. Tell me I'm not too late! I have a bunch of urgent stuff to go out!"

"You're just in time. I was teaching Indira how to use the franking machine. Otherwise, the mail would have been done and sent out." She took the envelopes from Mary. Still smiling, she said, "Indira, Mary works in the Redemptions department. Mary, Indira is a volunteer working in our department."

"I've heard about you—and they're all good things, by the way. I believe Peggy is very pleased with you."

"She's been of great help to us. You know how overworked we have been the past few weeks."

"Have you worked before in an investment firm?"

"Not at all. This is all so new to me."

"Indira was a costume designer in a repertory company," Val said.

"How interesting! Why don't you take up fashion design? It's a paying business," Mary said.

"I was never interested in designing clothes. I worked in the costumes department of a drama theatre because I love theatre. I used to act in a lot of stage productions in my school days."

"Why didn't you take up acting? You re so good looking!" Val said.

Indira paused before she said, "Things are not that simple in India. We come from a small city, and my husband's family is very orthodox ... you know, tradition-bound. My in-laws would die of shock if I started acting in plays."

"Well, it's different here, and you should try," Mary said.

"It's so difficult to even get a small job to make your ends meet here. They look for Canadian experience for everything! I'm sure it is so even in theatre. It may be very hard for a newly arrived immigrant to get a break."

"That's true," Val said.

"Unless you try, how will you know? To win the lottery you must first buy a ticket. Have a good one!" Mary said.

* * *

Days turned into weeks and weeks turned into months, and sedulous Indira, in the inseparable company of her seductive tresses, reported uncomplainingly to work.

"There are only four more weeks to go," Indira said, picking up a big mound of documents from her in-tray. "Soon, it will be back to plodding the pavements again."

"Don't say that," Sandy said. "Peggy's very impressed with you. Even if she's not able to offer you something in this office, she has connections. She may be able to get you a job somewhere or the other."

"If she can help me in anyway that will be great," Indira said. "All I am counting on is a good reference letter from Peggy."

"That's true. Even a good reference from Peggy will be most useful." Sandy said, "References are something on which prospective employers place a lot of importance in Canada."

"The weather's going to be glorious. What are you planning to do for the weekend, Sandy?" June asked.

"I have to attend my niece's birthday in Stoney Creek. We plan to spend the weekend there," Sandy replied.

"That's nice! How about you, Indira?"

Indira was silent for a few seconds before saying, "My husband has work this weekend. As you know, he works as a security guard."

"Tough luck," June said.

"We are happy that he has work at all. At this point in time, we think it's better to earn as much money as we can! We have the rest of our lives to splurge it."

"That's a nice way of looking at things," Sandy said.

* * *

It was never known what exactly Indira did on the weekend, but when she returned to work on the following Monday, she came all alone, meaning, devoid of any hair on her head. Her pate was bald, shaved clean. In one fell swoop, her crowning glory, it seemed, fell prey to an executioner's axe. It was a shock to see Indira without her waist-length hair. Despite her natural beauty, her appearance jarred on the senses. She looked like a female ET in a cheap Hollywood sci-fi flick.

"Holy smoke! What have you done to your hair?" Sandy said.

"It was becoming increasingly difficult to manage, so I got rid of it," Indira said, as if she had rehearsed the lines. "How do I look?"

"Lovely, my dear," Sandy said automatically, still dazed.

Her colleagues accepted Indira's reticence on the issue at face value and did not plague her with questions. But behind Indira's back, her hair, like King Charles' head, was a hot topic. The news spread like wildfire across the office.

That afternoon, Indira excused herself and left early. It was rumoured that she did so immediately after receiving a personal phone call.

The next morning, even the rest of Indira's body failed to report to work on time. Indira had never been late for work, not even by a few minutes even though she used public transit.

"Perhaps she missed the bus," Sandy said.

But an hour later, Sandy checked her voicemail. Nothing from Indira—it was so unlike her. Indira was a conscientious person. Sandy felt a disquiet she couldn't shrug off.

She called Peggy. "Indira has not come to work, and neither has she called. Do you know anything about it, Peggy?"

"I'm sorry, Sandy. I completely forgot! I meant to tell you. Indira will not be coming to work anymore."

"Anymore!" Surprise and a feeling of betrayal were evident in Sandy's voice. "But how can that be? Only yesterday she took on the job of updating the status report. She was supposed to handover the spreadsheet today!"

"That's inconvenient, I know," Peggy said, "but you'll have to manage on your own, Sandy."

"This is so sudden! Did she give you any reason for ditching us without a warning?"

"Well, I can't go into it right now, Sandy," Peggy said.

"You put me in charge of training Indira, Peggy. After all the time and effort I spent doing that, now you tell me without an explanation that Indira's not going to return! That's not fair!" Sandy said.

"I get where you're coming from. I'm sorry it's happened this way. I always like to give new immigrants a leg up. My parents too came as immigrants to Canada, and I heard about the hardships they faced. But with Indira, I was wrong. She's sincere and hardworking, all right, but our office is not the right fit for her."

"Really? I'm curious as to what could be the best fit for Indira," Sandy said.

"All I can say is that she's pursuing her dream. And I don't want the volunteer position we offered her to come in the way. Indira didn't want to reveal too much right now as things may not work out."

"I can't even begin to guess what kind of dream demands shaving off your lovely tresses!" Sandy said. "For a brief period, Indira brought mystery and mystique into our humdrum lives."

* * *

"When I saw her entering the office without a hair on her head I was stunned. I even forgot to greet her!" Sylvie the receptionist said, filling her bottle at the water cooler. "Imagine shaving off all that lovely hair." Sylvie herself had thin, short brown hair. It looked like a cap made from pelts of mice.

"Could it be for some medical reason?" Anna asked, heartily dipping into her Hungarian goulash.

"You mean some infection of her hair?" Sylvie asked. "Lice? Dandruff?"

"It could be cancer," June suggested, tucking into her mac-and-cheese. "People lose hair after chemotherapy, that sort of thing."

"You can't come to work if you're under treatment for cancer!" Yasmin said. She had finished her bowl of quinoa salad.

"One never knows, my dear," June said, continuing to eat her food with palpable delight. "She may not have WI— you know what I mean."

"She was not getting paid for her work, so how does it matter if she has Weekly Indemnity or not?" Anna said.

"She may not have company sponsored WI, but Peggy would have paid for EI. It's mandatory even for volunteers," Yasmin said.

The microwave beeped and Mary recovered her dish of clam chowder, and joined them. She said, "I saw a program about India on Discovery or some such channel. I believe women who lose their husbands have to shave their heads."

"How terrible," June said.

"It can't be that! She wouldn't turn up for work a day after her husband died!" Yasmin said.

"I asked Russell," Sylvie said. "He says people in India tonsure their hair when they visit holy shrines. He says the temples make a killing selling the hair to wigmakers around the world!"

Later, while trying to put together the spreadsheet, left half-done by Indira, Sandy said, "It's so unlike her to disappear like that, without a word."

"But it's nothing compared to the way her hair disappeared!" June said.

"Could it be possible she was wearing a wig all the while? Maybe she misplaced it or lost it or damaged it or something? Her long shiny tresses were quite unreal!" Val said.

"Who cares about her hair!" Sandy said with irritation. After all, she was the one who had to deal with the tasks Indira had left incomplete. "Misplaced her wig! Like leaving your umbrella behind on a bus! Really, Val. You're too much! Truth to tell, I am least interested in what has happened to her glorious locks."

"But everyone else in the office is," June told her. "Everyone has an explanation of their own. Even Russel had his worldly-wise take on it."

"What could it be? I am dying with curiosity," Sandy said blandly.

"He thinks there must be a more mundane reason for tonsuring her head."

"Like what?" Sandy asked.

"Well, that she could have shaved off her hair for a charitable cause," June said.

"Then why all the secrecy? Charity and publicity go together, right?" Val said.

"For me, the bigger mystery is why she left so suddenly, without even saying as much as a goodbye," Sandy said.

* * *

In the following month, the office planned a 'staff apprecia-
tion day.' It was a way by which management showed its
gratitude for its foot soldiers: the admin assistants. The
venue of the outing was an undisclosed location and none
of the office employees knew where it was, and truth to tell,
nobody cared. In fact, Peggy, who organised the event, was
the only one excited about the gradual build-up and the
mystery surrounding the party. Peggy had dyed her hair an
attractive auburn as if keeping in step with the season.

On the fateful Thursday afternoon, they went in a
chartered bus to the venue of the party. It turned out to be
a theatre: the Hummingbird Centre for the Performing
Arts. They had lunch at the restaurant and went to see a
play called *Star Trek, The Musical*.

"I don't know why we have to see this kind of kid stuff,"
Mary said. Her halo of hair had grown bigger, making her
look like a living saint.

"Never look a gift horse in the mouth," Sandy said. She
had coloured her hair ebony, as if in sympathy with the
missing Indira. The new hair colour made her look somehow younger and prettier.

"True. The only advantage I see is that you don't have
to do any work but still get paid. I think it's a good deal,"
June said. It was rumoured that June wanted to get rid of
her cranial hair—the only way to make the office take notice of you and your work.

"Don't forget the free lunch thrown in," Val said, who
had added ringlets to her hitherto lacklustre hair, as if
glamour was the new mantra in the office.

Later, when Peggy joined them, Mary said, as if wanting to redeem herself, "What a great choice, Peggy! My partner was telling me this one of the better sci-fi adaptations for the stage."

Peggy merely gave a knowing smile.

After the play began Peggy's herd watched the proceeding with varying degrees of enthusiasm. Sci-fi was not everyone's favourite. In fact, June could not even understand why the producers turned the original movie into a play, let alone go to the trouble of penning songs and setting them to music.

The stage set consisted mainly of the large cockpit of the starship, which was on a voyage to investigate a menacing space object. The dialogue seems stilted and they were treated to music inspired by classical pieces, mostly Brahms and Beethoven, but gingered up to an unrecognizable degree to sound like extraterrestrial claptrap.

Then came the scene that made the bored and restive group, sitting on either side of Peggy, sit up and take notice.

A door on the right-hand side of the stage slid open dramatically, and in walked an outlandish but somehow familiar figure. The enigmatic character's entrance, enhanced by the hodgepodge background score, seemed to eclipse everyone and everything on the stage. The character in the play was called Ilia, but there was no mistaking. It was Indira dressed in a loose pajama-top like garment, and little else. Her tonsured head, her most noticeable feature, shone with uncommon brilliance. Like some heavenly body.

A Mouthful of Sherry

It was while Mrs. Holmes sat on the verandah of her villa in St. Martin's Lea-upon-Thames, sipping a cup of Orange Pekoe, that she got the idea of how to commit murder and get away with it. Having all said and done, committing murder was easy. Escaping detection was the difficult part.

Her friend Katherine Atkinson sat opposite her, nibbling on a petit-beurre. "That Mr. Wentworth," her friend was saying, "running after girls young enough to be his granddaughters!"

While her friend prattled on, Mrs. Holmes' mind was elsewhere. She had always thought how ironic it would be if her husband were to die of unnatural causes and the person responsible for his death was to go scot-free. After all, Sherry had made such a career of catching criminals, earning fame and perhaps a fortune in the bargain.

Katherine leaned forward almost spilling tea onto her lap. She steadied the clattering cup and saucer, and whispered, "Hedwiga, I heard that Mr. Wentworth keeps some potions imported specially from Hong Kong in his bedroom."

Katherine was a small thin woman who lived in a red-tiled house down the lane. She claimed she hailed from Hamilton in Canada. She was Anglo-Indian and could pass for a white woman on a foggy day. She had met and married her English husband in Darjeeling in India where he had worked as a manager in a tea estate. Later they moved to Ontario as Paul Atkinson wanted to start a brewery there. But within a year he died of pneumonia, which had started as a common cold in late fall. Soon afterwards she moved to her husband's family home in England, a Victorian bungalow facing the Thames. An inveterate gossip, she had made more enemies than friends in the village. She lived alone and was rumoured to be wealthy. She would always say to Hedwiga, "You are my one and only true friend. Had you not been a wife of a well-to-do celebrity, I'd have left all my wealth to you." On one occasion she had added, unintentionally punning, "Maybe I still will."

Celebrity, most decidedly. Hedwiga wasn't quite sure about the "well-to-do" part. Sherry seemed to spend more money than he earned, chasing suspects and criminals all over the place. Hedwiga remembered the day she met Sherry for the first time. She was a teenager living in a small, impoverished village by the river Aar in central Switzerland. Skipping school one day, she had gone with two classmates to the riverbank to pick wildflowers. Imagine their horror when they came upon a man lying prone and insensible on the edge of the river. The three girls rushed into the river and pulled out the man. Hedwiga eagerly knelt and gave mouth-to-mouth. The man spluttered and came around. It was the very first time that Hedwiga had kissed a man full on his lips.

The man had turned out to be Sherlock Holmes! Hedwiga had not known then that Holmes had taken a tumble at the Reichenbach Falls only a few miles upstream. The girls gave him the apples and foul-smelling cheese they had brought for their picnic.

When Holmes appeared to regain some of his strength, Hedwiga took him to her house, which was a small stone cottage perched halfway up a hill. Her family was astounded to see an Englishman pop up in the fastness of Alpine mountains, having bloomed out of the water like some Venus in drag. Hedwiga's father, who was an avid reader of the international page of *Schweiz Zeitung* while waiting for his turn at the barber shop, recognized the famous profile, even as Sherlock Holmes sat down to eat the sauerkraut Hedwiga's mother had made.

"Don't you like it?" the lady asked, as Sherlock Holmes peered at the dish through his magnifying glass.

"It's not that, Frau Nicklausmeyer," said Sherlock in perfect high-country German which these simple Swiss folk found hard to follow. "I was merely deducing that whoever made this must be a German-speaking woman, a wife, a mother, and a cook."

"How clever of you!" Frau Nicklausmeyer said, faking admiration. She was good at grinding axes.

Sherlock stayed with them until he recovered completely. Afterwards he took a room in the village and began to live there instead of going back to England. The Nicklausmeyers were convinced that Sherlock Holmes was simply loaded. Why else would he appear in a Swiss newspaper? Switzerland was all about money and banking, so they encouraged their daughter to cultivate his friendship.

"But Mama, look at him. He must be ninety at least!"

"Use your head, Hedwiga," Frau Nicklausmeyer said. "The older your husband is, the less likely he's going to last. I wish I had got that advice when I was young. Now I'm stuck with your father, forever, it looks like."

Sherlock Holmes used to visit them regularly and sometimes played the violin to entertain Hedwiga. She could never recall when exactly she began to call him Sherry. It must have been the night he tweaked out a reedy *Moonlight Sonata*. Later they went out into the garden and kissed under the full moon. Hedwiga had a sneaking suspicion that it was the first time Sherry was kissing a woman, not counting of course the time he was lying half-dead on the riverbank.

It took two years of tireless efforts on the part of the entire Nicklausmeyer clan to make Sherry propose to Hedwiga. They were married at the English church at Meiningen, and soon afterwards they left for London. In the boat it became evident that while he had lots of stuff in his head, there was little to be said about his lower half. But she didn't let that worry her too much. After all, she hadn't married Sherry to make babies.

When they arrived in England, Sherry took up residence in the country instead of living at his lodgings in Baker Street. It must have been because of Mrs. Hudson. She mightn't have liked the idea of another woman monopolizing Sherry's attentions, thought Hedwiga. But her friend Katherine had another take on the matter.

"It's because of that Dr. Watson," she said. "There's something going on between the two of them."

But Katherine was wrong about Dr. Watson, Hedwiga was sure of that. Once, when Hedwiga had fallen ill, Sherry, who was busy pursuing a criminal in Denbighshire, sent Dr. Watson to look her up. Dr. Watson not only cured her of her illness, but he had some interesting antidotes for her acute loneliness.

After living for a year in England, it began to dawn on her that far from being rich, Sherry was neck-deep in debt. The house in the country had been used as collateral for a loan, and the lease on his place on Baker Street would expire in a couple of months, and Sherry didn't have the wherewithal to extend it.

"The only asset I have," Sherry admitted, "is my life insurance policy."

What a waste! All the collective efforts of the Nicklausmeyers had gone down the Rhine into the North Sea! Hedwiga was so mad that she wanted to pick up the violin and hit Sherry on his head with it. But she thought better of it; the violin was the only valuable thing in the house. You didn't have to be Sherlock Holmes, or his wife, to know it. The next day when she regained her composure, she went straight to the local library and borrowed a book on poisons. In the investigation that followed the murder that occurred at the villa, the police would question her about the volume, which was not yet returned to the library.

* * *

They had drunk the Orange Pekoe to the last drop and eaten all the petit beurres. Despite Hedwiga's unenthusiastic replies, Katherine was going on and on.

It must have been Katherine's talk about old Mr. Wentworth which started the train of thoughts in her mind. Not arsenic, not belladonna, but cantharides ... that's what she would use. But how does one get hold of it? Surely, one couldn't walk into Marks & Spencer and ask for a pound of it?

When Katherine had finally left in a flurry of goodbyes and kisses, Hedwiga sent a telegram to Holmes' Watson— now Hedwiga's Watson—a willing if witless collaborator in her fiendish scheme. She had promised him that when it was all over, they would together move to London in Ontario—Canada's winters notwithstanding. But in her heart, Hedwiga had no intention of keeping her word.

On the fateful evening, they were all present at the party: Holmes, Dr. Watson, Katherine, and Hedwiga herself. Hedwiga had bought a bottle of real sherry imported from Spain for the occasion. She had a connoisseur's taste for irony. They sat in the veranda and sipped their drinks appreciatively, except for Katherine who, not having a head for liquor, made a brave effort to swallow hers down.

The gentle breeze that wafted across from the Thames had a nip to it, reminding them that the summer would soon be over. Boats of every kind bobbed in the river, and now and then a steamer would bulldoze its way to London, sounding its horn stridently.

Katherine suddenly uttered a groan and fell forward, crashing on a Benares teapoy. When Sherry and Watson rushed to her side, it was already too late. Katherine died, exactly in the way Hedwiga had hoped for.

At the inquest, Hedwiga testified that she had wanted Holmes to have the doctored glass of sherry because the drug cantharides, better known as the Spanish fly, was reputed to be an aphrodisiac. But somehow the glasses had got mixed up and the dose meant for her husband was too much for a frail small woman like Katherine.

The verdict was death by misadventure. Contrary to the claims she had made when she was alive, Katherine was indeed a rich woman. She left all her wealth and property to her one and only true friend, Mrs. Hedwiga Holmes.

As they stepped out of the courthouse, Hedwiga said, "Westward Ho! London, here I come!"

"Darling," Holmes said, "London is to our south."

"You are always right about everything, Sherry!"

Asita's Valentine

1. *A Passage to India*

Asita sat in the crowded enclosure abutting a departure gate of Pearson Airport, hugging her capacious handbag to her bosom as if it were a child. The handbag contained their travel documents and the last of her money, prudently converted to US Dollars. On the seats on either side of her, her two daughters, Lavina and Kausalya, both aged five, lolled, rolled or bawled, depending on their state of mind. Periodically shushing her children, she waited for the announcement about the flight to London, the first leg of her long journey to Mumbai. The two airline employees already at the counter had been looking beaver-busy for quite some time, but the announcement about the start of boarding was not forthcoming.

To a casual observer (and many men observed Asita "casual-like" again and again because she was quite good-looking) her preoccupied, lacklustre eyes intimated if not fully expressed the turmoil in her heart. Leaving a husband and a country behind were not easy choices. What was worse, she was not even sure if she was doing the right thing. She may have been too impulsive, but she had to do something to put an end to the business-like coolness that had entered her relationship with her husband.

"I want to go to India for some time, to think things out," she had said.

All Raghu said was, "Take the children with you."

A voice whose clarity was lost in the airport's background susurration announced the departure of the flight, and invited only passengers in wheelchairs and families with small children to line up.

Yes, a single mother with two young children was handicapped, on the same footing as people in wheelchairs. She realized then that her real ordeal was just about to begin. Now, she had to take shelter in her parents' home in India, and share space, grudgingly given, with her brother and his family. Besides, she had no job, and not much money to speak of.

Asita dragged her two children, who wanted to make off in different directions, and ploughed her way through the crowd. There was no real line-up at the counter, just a human stockade made up of mostly young Indian software professionals returning home to have their batteries recharged. She showed their Indian passports and airline boarding passes to the gate agent. The man looked into her passport and then jerked his face up to scrutinize her face. Asita's heart thudded. *He has recognized me!* she thought. But he was only going through with his routine, and he glanced in turn at her daughters' faces too, before returning their travel documents.

2. *The Celestial Omnibus*

They shuffled through the passenger tunnel and entered the aircraft's belly through a narrow doorway, nodding at the cabin attendants who had taped guaranteed-not-to-shrink smiles on their lips. The economy-class seats were farther down the aisle, and she stumbled to their seat numbers, her hand luggage knocking against the seats along the aisle as she tried to shepherd her hyperactive children. They had a triad of seats adjoining a window all to themselves. The twins at once began to fight over the window seat, even though it overlooked the wing on the starboard side. Every time her daughters had a dispute, she was required to intervene with all the negotiating skills of Lester B. Pearson.

But since what she called "the incident," an event that had been splashed on the front pages of newspapers and was broadcast on every TV channel, her nerves had begun to fray, and she was becoming a little short on patience.

"I'm going take the window seat," she said firmly, though she would have preferred to sit by the aisle. "Now, move, the two of you. And I don't want to hear even a single peep."

When the last of the passengers filed past them, the cabin crew appeared in the aisles, battening down the overhead hatches. One of the cabin attendants took her position at the end of the aisle and, with a straight face, enacted her pantomime on emergency evacuation procedures. The twins might have enjoyed the performance had not the intervening headrests of the seats in front of them obscured their vision.

The aircraft began to roll backward and then forward, doing its little number on the tarmac as a warm up to the transatlantic hop. When it was finally airborne, a light-headed quiet settled on the cabin.

Three years ago, Raghu, the twins and she had come to Toronto on a similar plane from India—after a brief stop-over in London. They had led a comfortable and cushy life in India. Raghu had a well-paying job because he had a de-gree in management from a premier institute. But one day they realized that most of his father's property would go to his pampered, ne'er-do-well stepbrother. It was a move en-gineered by his stepmother, not out of any selfishness but out of fear for her son's future. It was then that Raghu de-cided to migrate to Canada.

Asita felt that Raghu should have stood up for his rights, at least for her and their children's sake, and not meekly decided to exile himself to Canada. But what man listens to his wife?

3. *A Room with a View*

In a field of vision shaped like a pizza slice, betwixt the wing and the fuselage, Asita saw the lights of Toronto re-cede and arc out of sight. Thanks to her meddlesome chil-dren, the small TV, stuffed into the back of the seat in front to her, came to life, offering a myriad of options for in-flight entertainment. Asita turned her face away.

When they first arrived in Canada, they took a small basement apartment without air-conditioning—the least expensive kind of accommodation available. It had only one window, high up in the wall, through which one could see a shard of sky. Even though it was the high noon of summer, they had to make do with artificial lighting so long as they were in the house.

But when Raghu got a job in a car parts plant, the first thing he did was to take out a mortgage and move into a cramped one-bedroom condo. From their balcony on the seventeenth floor, they could see a misty swathe of Lake Ontario in the distance. If Asita leaned out a little and slewed her eyes, she could even catch a glimpse of the CN Tower, pointing at the sky like a gigantic finger with an ill-fitting marriage band that had not slid all the way home.

Ensconced in their new home, Raghu and she could believe that life was beginning to improve. Once the twins started full-time school, she, too, could go to work. With the additional income, they could move into a townhouse close to where Raghu worked, and change the old, pre-owned Ford Focus they were using. They were settling well and felt less and less like immigrants as the days passed. Given a couple of more years, they would become not just Canadian citizens, but Canadians in every way.

4. *The Longest Journey*

One of the cabin attendants was pushing a dinner cart down the aisle at a snail's pace, dishing out drinks. On that fateful day, she too had been pushing a shopping cart between the narrow aisles of an Indian grocery store.

On the way home from the grocery, Raghu had stopped the car at a strip mall which had an Indian takeout called

The Golden Hind. It was the Sunday before Valentine's Day. He wanted to pick up chicken biryani for dinner—he and the children loved the aromatic rice cooked with pieces of spicy chicken.

"Want to come along?" Raghu had asked her. Asita's feet were aching. They had shopped both at the local super-market and the Indian grocery. She had kicked off her shoes and was in no mind to put them on and hobble after him.

"No, I'll wait in the car," she had said. What if she had meekly followed her husband to the restaurant? Would their seemingly placid and predictable lives have gone on forever?

Next to the Indian restaurant was a jewellery store. As she saw her husband's back disappearing behind the swing door, she wondered whether he would feel a twinge of ro-mance and dart into the jewellery store to buy her a small piece of nonsense for Valentine's Day. She would bet her last dollar that he wouldn't. Raghu had an indelible streak of fuddy-duddiness in him. He was adorable but not exciting at all, poor Raghu.

Theirs was a proper arranged marriage. Raghu's and her parents, though not friends, had known each other, and were distantly related. The horoscopes were perfectly com-patible, and the marriage was considered a match made in heaven. And it did look like that for the nearly seven years they spent as a married couple. Raghu, though not overtly loving, had a caring feeling for her. He was proud of her, proud of her looks. He felt he was responsible for her, in a proprietorial way.

The sounds of gunshots and breaking glass impinged on the thoughts of Asita who had chosen to remain in the car. Two men in masks rushed out of the jewellery store, brandishing firearms. They ran to a waiting automobile which was refusing to start. She could hear the starter grovelling. A door closed with a crash. The two men in masks, along with the driver of the getaway car, raced towards the car in which she sat. Though terrified, without knowing what she was doing, Asita leaned sideways in her seat and pulled out the key Raghu had left in the ignition. Dressed completely in black, the men would have looked fearsome even without their ski masks.

"Get outta the car!" the man nearest her side of the car thundered. Dutifully, Asita opened the passenger-side door.

"No!" the man who was yanking open the door on the driver's side yelled. "She's got the fucking key!"

Asita had her door half-open and was stepping out when the man pulled her back roughly into the car. Without uttering a word, he slapped her with the back of his hand, and prised the key out of her unprotesting palm. Asita felt a stinging pain on her left cheek. When the other two men had bundled themselves into the backseat, the car shot out like a cannonball. They travelled along the smaller city roads, zig-zagging through traffic. Asita heard police sirens in the nearby main streets, but no patrol car gave them chase.

Asita felt one side of her lower lip swell painfully and her mouth tasted salty with blood. She turned her head to reach out for the box of tissues she kept at the back of the car.

"Don't look back," the driver said. "For your own safety."

"I want some tissues," she said.

"Zack, can you help her?"

"Here," Zack grunted. The driver took the box and offered it to Asita. "Take it," he said. He had yanked off his mask, revealing a boyish clean-cut face with steel-grey eyes.

He might have been a nerdy student rather than a hoodlum fleeing from a scene of crime. As she grabbed a few tissues and dabbed her mouth, he said, "I'm sorry for hitting you."

His apology for some reason made her want to cry. And for the same unknown reason she felt less frightened too. They were on a rural highway heading west. The traffic had thinned to a trickle, and isolated homes and farmhouses along the road slid by. The landscape was flat and expansive, and Asita saw glimpses of frozen ponds.

"Step on it, Josh. Or we'll never make it to Fred's place before dark."

"I'm doing my best, Bert. This car must be a hundred years old."

"Lady," Zack said, "couldn't your man afford a better car?"

"My husband works in a factory; he doesn't loot jewellery shops. Anyways, your car wouldn't even start."

"Did you hear that, Zack?" Josh said with a laugh.

"The lady has spirit," Zack said. "Where are you from, Mexico?"

"That's enough," Josh said.

Asita thought of her children and was relieved that this was happening to her and not to them, or in their company. She would have been half-crazed with worry if it were they who were spirited away. Raghu was known to be cool and methodical. He could cope with every emergency. Also, it would do him good to take care of the children for once.

They drove for hours before Josh brought the car to a halt at a trail that led into the woods. "Get out of the car," he said. "We'll have to leg it from here."

It was already getting dark, and a cold breeze was whistling through the denuded maples and spruces. She could hear scurrying sounds in the undergrowth. As they walked over the uneven ground of the woods, covered with patches of snow and ice, Asita slipped and fell into a puddle of wet, melting snow. Josh helped her rise to her feet. He took her arm and piloted her along the invisible trail. Shivering with cold, she shambled alongside them. After trekking for twenty minutes, they came to a copse, in the middle of which stood a cabin. There was a small light glowing inside. Josh kicked the unlocked door open, and they all filed in. Josh led Asita to a small room and said, "Stay here and don't make a noise. If all goes well, we'll free you tomorrow."

There was a chair and a pallet which had been slept in. It was bone-chillingly cold, even colder than what it had been outside, and her wet clothes made it worse. Josh returned with a small stove. "This will keep you warm," he said, and left.

She spent the night sleeping fitfully, and in her sleep, she thought she heard men talking outside her window. Every time she awoke, her fear, verging on panic, returned. But somehow, the behaviour of the jewel thieves didn't seem violent or dangerous. She got the feeling that she was being seen as nuisance rather than a threat. Their heist was a success; they only had to share their loot and disappear into their netherworld, far from the reach of the police.

5. *The Eternal Moment*

It must have been early in the morning, when Josh knocked on the door and entered the room. It was pitch dark outside, but the birds were atwitter, gossiping amongst themselves as if their lives depended on it. What kind of birds wanted to stay back in Canada and not escape to Florida for the winter? Patriotic ones, she supposed. Loons!

"We'll have to leave now," Josh said. She got up, smoothed her dress, and tried to discipline her hair. She put on the coat she had hung on the chair-back to dry and followed him. The two of them began to walk in the direction from which they had come last evening. Her fear returned irrationally. *Is he taking me to a lonely spot to kill me?*

"Where are your ... eh ... friends?" Asita asked. She had almost said conspirators.

"Zack doesn't like your car," Josh said. "They're trying to arrange for another."

"Good for them."

When they reached the car, Josh had to turn the key many times, to cajole the car to life.

"The battery is good, whatever Zack might say of the car."

"Thank you. My husband will be overjoyed with your assessment."

Josh ran the engine on idle for a few minutes and then steered the car out of the woods. The day was beginning to lighten, and Josh drove over roads which looked unfamiliar to Asita. After an hour or so, they reached the outskirts of a town. In the distance, she could see a clutch of tall office blocks.

"That's St. Catharines," he said.

They sat in silence. Josh looked as though waiting for something to happen.

"Do you drive?" he asked suddenly.

"Yes," she said, a feeling of partisanship stirring within her. "Do you want to hire me as the new getaway driver?"

"I want you to take this car and go home."

"I don't have the licence to drive on highways."

"I'll tell you what: You go into the town and give yourself up to the police."

"Give yourself up, indeed!"

"Whatever. You drive three blocks down the road until you hit the main road. Then you turn right and drive for a mile and you will see a police station on your right."

"What about you? Are you planning to go off on foot?"

"Don't worry about me," he said. "Here, I've got something for you."

He reached out for his black swag bag and burrowed his hand into it. He pulled out a ring. "Happy Valentine's Day!" he said.

She took it in her hand. It was a fourteen-karat gold ring with an outline of a heart made with small rubies and diamonds.

"When I saw it, I knew who to give it to," Josh said.

"I can't take it," Asita said, tossing the ring back to him. "It's stolen property. If I take it, I'll have to join you in your prison cell."

"That's not a bad idea. But nobody's going to catch me." He leaned over and kissed her on her lips. Asita was taken aback. Other than her husband, nobody had kissed her, and his kisses were like a warm poultice pressing on her mouth. Whereas Josh's mouth held hers like a limpet, until she had to roughly push him away.

A shiny Toyota Camry rolled to a stop on the opposite side of the road. Zack was at the wheel. When he saw her, he grinned and waved his hand.

"It looks as if Zack has learnt his lesson," Josh said, looking at the condition of the car. "Take care!" He ran across the road and got into the car. No sooner did the door shut than the car sped away, leaving nothing behind but a doppler echo of a receding car ...

And a memory of an unpremeditated but passionate kiss.

6. *Where Angels Fear to Tread*

When she reached the police station, they took a statement from her and sent her to the hospital for first-aid. When Raghu arrived with a family friend, an identikit picture of Josh had been completed. She was secretly pleased that the man in the portrait did not resemble Josh very much. It had captured his likeness to a certain extent, but not his character.

When they stepped out, they were met with a fusillade of flashbulbs. She became prime time news. Though she had kept her mouth shut all through except for saying, "No comments," long and exciting stories were written about her adventure.

For the first few days, Raghu had been understanding, kindness personified. Then one day out of the blue he lobbed the question: "Did the doctors examine you thoroughly?"

"No, they treated me for the bruise on my mouth."

"Did the gangsters beat you?"

"No, I was slapped once, that's all."

"You were in such a state. Bedraggled and bruised and all."

"I had slipped and fallen into a puddle. The small cut on my lower lip was already healing."

"Would you like to see a doctor?"

"Whatever for?"

"You had a traumatic experience. You spent a night in the company of three thugs."

"They did nothing to me. They were only intent on making a quick getaway."

"I know it's embarrassing to speak about it. But a doctor will keep it confidential."

"Believe me, Raghu, I've *not* been raped."

Raghu looked unbelieving. Asita felt an upsurge of anger, alloyed with a sense of humiliation. "Go to hell!" she barked, and jumping out of the bed, she went and slept in the children's bedroom. Soon Asita regretted her hasty decision, but she did not know of a way to repair the damage. Raghu was unbending, and their relationship was not the same anymore.

There were stories going around in their social circle about Asita being gang-raped when in captivity. Asita suspected Ajay, the friend who had accompanied Raghu to the St. Catharines police station, for starting the rumours. Whenever they met, Ajay would not miss an opportunity to make loaded comments accompanied by a smirk on his face. One evening, as they were waiting for Raghu who was delayed in the office to return, Ajay made a pass at her.

"Keep your hands to yourself!" Asita had said.

"Why? You prefer only white men's cocks now, is it?"

"Get out of my house!"

When Raghu returned less than half an hour later, Asita told him of the incident.

"What else can you expect?" was Raghu's response.

Even in mythology, the esteemed heroine Queen Sita, despite her royal status and divine antecedents, had to face public contumely and spousal skepticism after she was rescued from her abductor. How could things be different for a mere middle-class mortal like Asita?

Even after she returned to the master bedroom, and laid herself down on the king-size bed, there seemed to be no change in Raghu's attitude. For years they had shared a commonality of purpose, having trodden a path whose direction and goal was mapped out for them by centuries of tradition. Now, fate had derailed them.

7. *The Life to Come*

After cooling their heels in Heathrow for two hours, they boarded the Air India flight to Mumbai.

Five hours out, Asita saw, from the vantage point of her window seat, black smoke billowing from one of the engines on the wing. The other passengers noticed it too, and a collective hubbub rose like a tidal wave. Muffled screams punctuated confusion and consternation.

Soon the authoritative voice of the pilot-in-command, broke over the PA system: "We are having a problem with one of the four engines of the plane. I request all passengers to fasten the seat belts and remain calm. We don't foresee an immediate emergency, but we will be closely monitoring the situation."

In the event, the plane was diverted to a disused airstrip in a remote corner of Kazakhstan (or was it Uzbekistan?). Once they deplaned, instinctively, she thought of calling Raghu. But she thought better of it, imagining his indifferent response: "What do you want me to do?"

He would come to know of their plight soon enough from the online editions of Indian newspapers he read every day.

She called her father instead, and immediately regretted it. He was the proverbial mother hen, and his alarmed reaction needed so much placating that it unnecessarily taxed her already frayed nerves.

Asita and her children, along with the other two hundred-odd passengers, waited for eight hours in a barn-like terminal building without water and proper food for a relief plane to come. And when it did, it took another two hours for all the passengers to board, and the plane to finally take wing.

When the plane reached Mumbai, it kept circling over the city like a reconnoitring hawk. At long last, it lowered its nose and dove, like a predator bird that had spotted an appetizing prey.

At that moment, inexplicably, Asita was overcome with desolation. She did not want the plane to land in India. She wanted it to make a U-turn and return to Canada. She ought to have been happy at the thought of visiting her parents. She had not seen them for three years. Yet, she felt an ache in her throat, and she was close to breaking down.

Was this all there was to a marriage? Raghu and she had gone around the sacred fire seven times, symbolizing a union for eternity. In their case, it had lasted exactly seven years. What did Raghu feel about their marriage? About her? Wouldn't he miss the children? Can he live all by himself forever, without his family?

There was a moment when she wanted to subject herself to a medical examination, just to please Raghu. But if she did that, she knew, she would never have been able to look at herself in the face.

By now, Raghu must have come to know of their aerial misadventure. What were his feelings? Wouldn't he be overcome with concern for her and the children—especially the children?

When they entered the terminal building, Asita pulled out her mobile and switched it on. She wanted to call Raghu ... and tell him what? That they were safe and not to worry?

The phone was already trying to sniff out a compatible network. Asita hesitated. What if Raghu rebuffed her?

Even as she was thinking, the phone began to ring. The screen showed up a four-letter word: Home. It was Raghu calling. She pressed the green button.

Only connect.

Acknowledgements

I thank Mississauga Arts Council for conferring me with their much-coveted 'Marty' for the stories contained in this volume.

I'm grateful to Michael Mirolla and Connie McParland of Guernica Editions for continuing to repose their faith in my story-telling abilities. I also thank my editor Kulamrit Bamrah for making my collection a readable and, I hope, enjoyable experience.

I'm forever beholden to my long-suffering family, who, despite not having any taste for literature, cope with an idiosyncratic writer every day of their lives.

About The Author

Pratap Reddy immigrated from India to Canada in 2002. Holding down a job as an underwriter in an insurance firm provided him the sustenance to pursue his dream of becoming a writer. He has authored two books, *Weather Permitting & Other Stories* and *Ramya's Treasure,* both on themes of immigration. He is currently working on a book of verse and a novel tentatively titled *Praful's Errands,* both of which—he's happy to add—stay clear of the topic of immigration. He serves on the board of *Diaspora Dialogues,* a non-profit organization which supports new writing and emerging writers.

MIX
Paper
FSC® C100212

Printed by Imprimerie Gauvin
Gatineau, Québec